WAR PLAN RED VOLCANO

THE WAR IN
2029

IRA TABANKIN

The War in 2029
"War Plan Red Volcano"
Copyright June 2025
Ira J. Tabankin
Knoxville, TN 39720
Cover by 100 Covers

Dedication:

This book is dedicated to my wife and true love, Patricia.

Thanks

I want to thank my beta readers, who helped me with their knowledge, comments, and encouragement. I want to thank Cassandra Kardeke, who edited and made this edition possible.

Note:

Please note that this isn't a politically correct novel. Please recognize that artistic license is used throughout this story. Any tense disparities are the author's view of the story as it's written.

Work of Fiction:

This is a work of fiction. Names, characters, businesses, places, events, and incidents are either the products of the author's imagination or used in a fictitious manner. Any resemblance to actual persons, living or dead, or actual events is purely coincidental.

A Note on Punctuation:

Much of this story is a conversation between people; when we speak, we don't do so in the same manner as the written word. Pauses in the written word aren't usually there when we talk to each other. As such, the punctuation used in conversations is written as people speak, not as it would be in a written paragraph.

Copyright June 2025

Note on Names:

The names of the respective countries' leaders in this story are the same, and all the supporting staff have fictional names. The embedded map was created before President Trump changed the names of the military bases.

Prologue

The Chinese are a patient race. From 713 to 1820 CE, they were the world's most powerful country. They had developed gunpowder and rockets. They built a wall to keep the outsiders out. The Chinese Communist Party (CCP) took control of China in 1949. They defeated the Nationalists who crossed the straits and made their home on the island of Taiwan. The PRC (People's Republic of China) considered Taiwan to be part of the PRC. Their present president, Xi pledged to return Taiwan to the people of China. They pledged to be the world's sole superpower on or before 2049. A hundred years after the CCP gained control of China.

The CCP's war planners developed a war plan they called "*Red Volcano*," as the military had to climb a large mountain for them to break America's back and allow them to still be the breadbasket of China. Like all war plans, '*Red Volcano*' was updated based on the degree of readiness of the PLA (People's Liberation Army) and the condition of their main opponent, the United States of America. They knew that when, not if, America fell, Europe and South America would fall in line, and would take orders from Beijing.

The PLA had a ringside seat to the ongoing war in Ukraine because they helped supply Russia with weapons and technology that the West had blocked Moscow from obtaining. The PLA was surprised how quickly both the Ukrainians and the Israelis managed to develop and deploy new weapons. They were surprised by the mass use of suicide drones by every entity engaged in the wars. They were surprised how quickly the Ukrainians and Russians installed cage armor to protect their tanks from drones that attacked the top, the thinnest armor on a tank.

The Chinese planners knew that the one opponent they had to take down at the start of the war was the American Navy. While the PLAN (People's Liberation Army Navy) had more ships than the American Navy, they didn't have the experience of operating under the pressure of war. The Americans gained critical experience defending their high-value target, their carriers in the Red Sea. The Chinese also studied what happened when the American ships ran out of missiles. The Chinese Minister of Defense smiled. "That is their weakness, and it's where we will strike. Most of their destroyers play defense to protect their carrier, which is their offensive arm.

Notice what happens when they run out of missiles and study the cost ratio of the drone to the Americans' defensive missiles. The Iranian drones cost between 20 and 50,000 American dollars. The cost of America's defensive missiles is between 2.5 and 5 million dollars. Not even America can continue to build enough missiles to defend against thousands of drones. The cost of one of their SM 6 missiles equals the cost of at least 125 drones."

An Admiral looked at the Minister. "Sir, those destroyers only carry a maximum of one hundred missiles."

"Excellent, you're beginning to see their weakness and our strength. Remember Sun Tzu's teachings. 'Know yourself and know your opponent. Preparation is key. Timing and Opportunity.' The key to our victory lies in his teachings. Timing is going to be handed to us; it will be the window of opportunity we will use to defeat the Americans by turning their strength into a weakness. We will practice the attack until we can operate it in the dark with our eyes closed.

"The Americans established the timing, we will allow them to set the stage while we walk away with the prize, the prize is that China will be the sole superpower when the curtain falls."

The planning staff had started with one plan that relied on a counterforce nuclear surprise attack on America's largest military bases and on the Minuteman silos by China's secret stealth bombers. The Chinese Ministry of State Security (MSS), their version of America's CIA, bribed two members of the Pentagon's planning staff so they could learn how America would respond to a Pearl Harbor-type of nuclear attack.

The MSS learned they had to change their plan because their spies told them that if China launched nuclear missiles directed at America, America would respond with an overwhelming amount of force. The Chinese weren't sure they could survive such a counterpunch by the Americans. The Chinese knew that if they managed to take out the Minuteman silos, they would still have to face 840 Trident warheads that were accurate enough to be considered a first-strike weapon. They knew America kept some bombers on alert, armed with at least twenty nuclear weapons around the clock. The planners reviewed their other options.

The MSS told Xi their war plan, 'Red Volcano, was a nod to the sacrifices China was going to have to endure in order to be successful and break America's back. When Xi first reviewed the plan, he was both surprised and worried that the Americans weren't so dumb as to allow the first phase of the plan to be implemented.

Xi decided to observe the Americans' reaction as the PLA and MSS launched phase 1 of the plan. He watched the Americans doing something he thought was impossible. He had placed a large bet with the Director of the MSS that the Americans would never allow phase 1 of the plan to go forward. He told his friend there was no way they would sell out, and yet they did. He ordered that the plan could never be placed in an electronic file, so it couldn't be hacked by the Americans who'd formed a top echelon hacking department at the NSA at Fort Meade, Maryland. Xi told the planning group he had selected the date to destroy America. January 20, 2029. The date the new American president would be sworn into office. He timed the attack to happen when the new president placed his hand on the bible, an event televised around the world. Clocks didn't have to be coordinated, as everyone would see the event in real time.

At the time of the inauguration of America's 48th President in the areas west of the international date line where U.S. assets are deployed, the PLA outnumbered U.S. forces about 12-to-1 in modern fighter jets (including 5-to-3 in fifth-generation aircraft) and 3-to-1 in maritime patrol planes. In bombers, the PLA's fleet of 225 manned bombers faced no competition in the region. On the seas, the PLA had a 3-to-1 advantage in aircraft carriers and amphibious ships, more than a 6-to-1 lead in advanced submarines, and a staggering 9-to-1 advantage in modern multi-warfare combat ships.

China had invested billions in the development and deployment of high-technology weapons, such as railguns, a technology America had given up on after leading the world. The PLAN also had heavily invested in lasers to shoot down missiles and to blind pilots. The buildup had cost China over $2 trillion. It was a price Xi agreed to pay, as the payoff meant the accomplishment of the master plan twenty-one years sooner than anyone thought possible.

The chess pieces were placed on the board, and the Chinese waited like a coiled snake for the moment to attack. Sometimes 'Lady Luck' smiles on you, and sometimes she laughs. This time she smiled on the Middle Kingdom.

Chapter 1

The War Plan, '*Red Volcano.*' January 2020

China had studied how the Americans voted. They needed to ensure the existing president was defeated so they could lay the foundation for their war plan. In a gray, chilly early morning meeting between the Director of the MSS, Shingho, and Xi, the president of China, Shingho unveiled his plan. Xi listened for ten minutes before he raised his hand to silence Shingho.

Xi shook his head. "If I understand the initial part of your plan correctly, you're proposing we create IDs for tens of thousands of people who either don't live in the American states and may not even exist to ensure we have sufficient votes for our candidate, or we create the ballots and add or replace the real mail ballots with ours? Won't the Americans realize there are too many ballots in those areas?"

"Sir, that's the beauty of our plan. We've studied the percentage of people who typically vote, and we stay within a couple of percentage points of that number. Their Presidential elections always show increases in the percentage of people who vote. This election is bound to have more people voting by mail than any other because of their fear of COVID that spread across their country and the world. All we have to do is add sufficient votes in their so-called 'swing states' and the election will fall into our laps. We cannot allow the current president to win another term. After he is defeated, we need to make sure he is soiled goods, arrested, his home invaded by their federal police, and his privacy invaded. We ruin him as a candidate and as a man. We use their legal system to bankrupt him. Maybe the court will find him guilty and send him to prison, where we can arrange for a fatal accident to happen to him. Then we'll never have to worry about him again."

Xi slowly walked around the large, polished mahogany conference table. He stopped across from his friend, the Director of the MSS. "Old friend, I hear you and I understand your plan, however, I see a greater danger in attacking him. We might make him a martyr, thus ensuring he runs and wins a second term. We both know the American public wants a change. We can make them believe they need what the old man will be selling. Once he's elected, our people will control the country. We can only continue this for one term because people on the inside will talk."

Shingho smiled. "We have made plans for anyone who even thinks of speaking…"

Xi nodded. "Make it look like an accident. I don't want to read a news report that so-and-so committed suicide by shooting himself in the back of his head twice."

"That insult hurt. My people are like hers. She believes she can get away with anything because the American media is on her side. They hate their present President so much that they'd support the devil over him. Their media does our bidding, and because we own their media, their people will vote how we want them to."

Xi smiled. "Her time will come, only not yet. We may need to expose her to give their reporters something 'hot' to report on, versus if one manages to figure out their president can't tie his own shoes, and if not watched around the clock, he will wander into traffic. The pandemic provided the perfect cover for him. He has to stay healthy for the election. Once he is elected, we can move to phase two and begin our land purchases. What about their Senators and key reporters? How have you protected us from them slipping up?"

"We have arranged to make generous donations to state senators in the key states so they will count mail-in ballots even if they arrive after the normal close of voting. We will know the count before it's announced, so we'll know how many mail-in ballots we'll need to swing the election. We are also making donations from our people in the country and some companies we own. We have excellent blackmail material on the reporters on CNN and MSNBC. If they dared speak what they know, they would be ruined and in some cases, they would lose their families."

Xi walked around the table again. "Are you one hundred percent positive we can't be caught? Positive enough that the lives of your family and all of your relatives are at risk if we're caught?"

"Sir, I lay my life and my family at your feet. I am one hundred percent positive that our plan will work. May I show you something?"

"What is it?"

"Sir, here is a mail-in ballot, not usually used till now because of COVID. Here is our copy of the form. Can you spot which one is ours and which one is theirs?"

Xi held the two ballots up to the lights. He traced the print with a damp finger, and he smiled. He held up a ballot. "This is ours."

"Sir, that is their ballot. Ours is the one on the table in front of you."

"How did you manage to get one of their actual ballots? How did you reproduce it so convincingly?"

Shingho smiled. "Sir, we have over eight hundred very loyal people working in their post office. It was child's play to grab a few of their ballots. We scanned the document like we scan different currencies. We reproduced it even with the signature so perfectly that not only could you not spot which one was ours, but when a group of Americans looked at the ballots, every one of them picked ours as the real ballot."

"How could you manage to show these two to the American counters without risking our plan?"

"Our people had FBI ID cards. They looked and acted like American agents. We have thousands of hours of recordings of how they dress and act. The silly Americans saw their ID cards and badges, and their eyes told them our agents were real. We used other focus groups to see if they could pick out the counterfeit bills we are about to line their politicians' pockets with. Here are matching American twenty and fifty-dollar bills. Can you tell the difference?"

Xi picked up each bill. He ran his fingers over the front and back. He held them up to the light. He had one of his aides bring him a portable UV light to study the bills. After twenty minutes, Xi smiled and held up four bills. "These are the real American bills. You did very well. You almost fooled me, but there is a difference in the feel of the bills."

Shingho nodded. "Please ask your aide to bring you a few American dollars so you can compare them to the ones you're holding."

Xi was getting frustrated. "I am not a child. I made my choice. Did I shame you by selecting the counterfeit bills?"

"Mr. President, all six were counterfeit. Here are real American bills, what do you say now?"

Xi called in five members of his staff. "Choose which are real American bills and which ones are counterfeit. Those who choose correctly will be given a reward."

The aides felt each bill; all were folded and dirty. When Xi said, "Time is out, select."

Four of the five selected the Chinese counterfeit bills. The fifth selected the real American bills. Xi asked the one who had selected the actual American bills. "What made you select the real ones?"

"Sir, all of the bills felt and looked real. When the other four decided to select the bills on your left, I decided to be the outlier and selected the other bills. Honestly, I could not feel or see any difference. I honestly couldn't tell the difference between the two."

Xi smiled. "Take the bills, all of them. Thank you." He dismissed the other four with a wave of his hand to the security guards who nodded. They'd understood their silent orders. The four who chose as a group would die this morning in a group, and their families would be billed for the cost of the bullets and the cost to bury their loved ones.

Shingho nodded to Xi. "Sir, are you convinced now?"

"Why didn't you print their hundred-dollar bills?"

"Their hundred-dollar bill is the one that has the highest number in circulation. While it's the bill with the highest circulation, the criminals and cartels account for the largest percentage of the bills. When a one-hundred-dollar bill is presented at a bank or store, they are almost always checked. No one checks their twenty- or fifty-dollar bill. We have also printed their five and ten-dollar bills in addition to their rare but still in circulation two-dollar bill. By not printing hundred-dollar bills, we removed a high risk of being caught. We are also helping the Americans experience a period of rapid inflation due to the mass dumping of hundreds of billions into their economy through the programs of their soon-to-be new president."

"Who are we paying off?"

"Six state senators in the state of Pennsylvania. Four in Michigan, eight in Ohio, nine in North Carolina, and nine in Georgia. By ensuring our candidate wins these swing states, he will win the election. We have vetted his new staff, and we own most of them. They will open their borders, thus allowing the PLA to install bases in their country. We have also made sure six senators are on our payroll. We've been paying them with these bills, so it doesn't affect our position regarding the debt we carry, and we will demand repayment shortly before the war begins. When the time comes and you issue the 'go' code, everything and everyone will be in their positions to attack a sleepy America."

"I like it. Please proceed. Once we knock America to her knees, her people will demand that they not get into a war with us. We will threaten to use our nuclear weapons if they attack us. We will hit them where and when they least expect. If phase one succeeds, and it looks like it will. When the time comes, we will have knocked most of their military off of the board."

The two shared a cup of fresh tea that had just been delivered to the conference room. Xi smiled. "I can see your hand in this plan. It is like you. The Americans will watch the swearing in of their new president only to learn that our troops are already there and have taken over the Americans' most important military bases. It is crucial that our candidate wins the Presidency both in 2020 and 2024. He is so old that he won't remember giving permission to his staff to issue executive orders that they wrote and signed with the president's autograph machine. By the time he clears his head long enough to question why everyone is complaining about his closed border, which is really one that is wide open. I want to strike and take America off the board when they swear in their new President on January 20, 2029."

Shingho nodded. "We will strike from where they least expect it and when they least expect it. Sun Tzu taught us, 'All war is based on deception.' We are acquiring farms near their key military bases. They will be our forward operating bases from where we will launch the attack that will leave only one of us the winner, and it will be us. They'll know what's happening to them before our rockets tear them apart."

Xi nodded his head. "We will give them plenty of issues to focus on so they don't look at what we're doing. We will arrange for Jung-un to launch a massive strike on Seoul. The Indians and Pakistanis will have one of their wars, and to add some additional confusion to the Americans' list of problems, Iran will order Hamas to strike Israel, and the Houthis will strike Saudi Arabia and every ship in the Red Sea. Sixty percent of the world's oil travels in tankers using the Red Sea.

"The American military will be stressed more than they were in both World Wars. As the Americans say, they won't know whether to shit or go blind. We'll give the Houthis a handful of EMP warheads to install in their cruise missiles. They'll be able to cripple one of America's carrier strike groups. They've reduced their military from the days of Reagan to the levels of just before the First World War. While we grow strong, they grow weak. Soon, the world will see that the Americans are a paper tiger, and we are the rightful rulers of the world."

Xi paused to sip some water. "We will offer to produce their steel, refined nickel, and aluminum for less than they could produce it for. They won't be able to exist in the twenty-first century without us. We control their rare earth minerals, most of their medications, and to make sure they are dependent on us, once the new president is elected and takes office, he will sign a series of executive orders that will block them from drilling for oil and gas or from mining the minerals they need to build their advanced systems. We'll also accelerate the rate of farmland we own, and then we'll be able to control the food that grows in their own country. The survivors will work for us. We will use them to help us conquer the rest of the world."

The two toasted the plan. Shingho committed to hand-delivering the weekly updates in person. Xi reminded him that no electronic records should be kept where America's NSA might sniff them out and turn the plan against them.

Phase one of their plan worked perfectly. Their candidate won, the borders were wide open, the defense budget was cut, and billions were spent on DEI racial issues. The American Secretary of Defense walked around wearing a plastic face shield. No one took him seriously. As the election of 2024 loomed, Xi called his war council together to announce Phase two of *Red Volcano* was four years away and with it, the conquest of America.

The committee applauded and raised their tea to Xi.

Chapter 2

Beijing, November 2024

After the success in 2020, Xi decided it was time to announce the next steps of the plan to the Central Military Committee. Xi assembled his most trusted advisors, the country's Central Military Commission: the director of MSS (He Shingho), the commanding general of the PLA (General Xi Ho Jinping), and commanding general of the PAP (People's Armed Police) and the Militia of China (General Xen Xong). Also invited was the Minister of Foreign Affairs, Wang Yi.

Xi asked Shingho to brief the members on the plan and their responsibilities to ensure its success. They knew if they failed, they and their families would be executed or sent to a labor camp under the charge of accepting bribes. The charges weren't really necessary because when Xi told Shingho to have someone arrested, the charges and trial were meaningless, and the accused was usually never seen again.

Jinping stood and was recognized by Xi. "Mr. President, may I speak frankly and only in this room?"

"General. Whatever you say inside this room will never be repeated. If you see a weakness in the plan, this is the time and place to speak it. All must know if we are planning for failure."

All of the other members held their breath; they knew Jinping had just committed suicide. A fate none wished to join the General in.

"Mr. President, generals, minister, and Director of MSS," (who was the only one in the room Jinping really feared. He knew he and the President had disagreements, but behind closed doors, they managed to work out their differences, and plans were always improved. Xi respected the General and was one of a very small number who had the 'balls' to tell the President he was wrong.) "Thank you for explaining where some of my best troops disappeared to. I believe *Red Volcano* is a good plan. I like the name volcano. A volcano shoots lava and burning rocks miles away. It destroys everything in its path. The PLA will do the same, we will use the war plan to destroy the Americans.

"However," (Everyone in the room wanted to crawl under the table when they heard the word 'however.' A word that usually carried the death penalty for speaking out against one of the Party's plans. They knew Xi held total power and could have all of them shot in minutes.) "After studying the failed Russian invasion of Ukraine, I believe we must change our order of battle and change the way the PLA is organized."

Xi's face reddened. "General, are you trying to say you want to retire? If so, just say the word and you will be relieved of your position."

"Sir, I am not asking to be relieved of my position. I would like to point out a couple of issues we should review before we enter into a war with the Americans."

Xi smiled like he knew what was going to be said, and he had already rehearsed his response. "Please continue."

Jinping bowed to Xi. "Sir, thank you. Let's remember the Russians planned to capture the capital of Ukraine in one week, ten days at the outside. What started in 2014 and accelerated in 2022 has been a failure, and we're helping them by giving them some of our equipment. Their poor performance underlies the problem in their army, ours, North Korea's, and others. The weakness and reason for their failure isn't their weapons, it's that war decision-making can't be centralized. The Ukrainian army is like the Americans, decentralized. Compare the progress the Americans had against

Iraq in their first Gulf War, and the Russians, who watched but didn't learn anything from it. It isn't a difference of weapons; it's how the decisions in the field are made.

"Look at how quickly Ukraine changes policies, makes, and deploys new weapons and defenses. Even the Russians, who bragged about their unstoppable hypersonic missiles, have watched their new weapons being intercepted and stopped before they hit their targets. They're learning. The Ukrainians are learning and adopting every day. In the middle of a war, they designed and deployed an unmanned suicide boat that sank a Russian cruiser. The Black Sea, once a Russian lake, is now a no-man's zone.

"The answer isn't new equipment, it's training and allowing the NCOs (Noncommissioned Officers, usually sergeants and warrant officers) to make decisions. The Americans train this into their NCOs. They are given an outline of a battle plan and told to accomplish their goals. They aren't told to report back every hour. If they did, they'd report their radio had been hit. Europe has studied the war because it's on their front yard, and they are starting to train how the Americans fight. Do you think the captain of one of their destroyers calls his admiral asking permission to sink a target? It's up to the ship's captain, and not usually even a captain in rank.

"Placing people close to the Americans' bases was a brilliant move. Getting the Americans to open their borders so our people could just walk in was also brilliant. I bow to you and Director Shingho. I was going to bring this up at our bi-annual meeting, but given that we are going to strike at the Americans' soft inner belly, we should change how those troops are trained and make sure the NCOs know they will be responsible for victory or defeat, and sir, the PLA doesn't lose."

The room was completely silent. Xi looked into the eyes of his generals and department heads. He mentally told himself he had to replace them before they launched 'Red Volcano.' There was one man with the guts to stand up and speak truth to power. He needed more people like Jinping. "General, please remain after we are finished here. I would like to hear more about the reorganization you have mentioned."

Xi nodded and smiled. The others thought his smile meant they wouldn't be seeing Jinping again. When the room was cleared, Xi looked at Jinping. "Do you really believe we are too centralized, and it can be a reason why we'd lose?"

"I do. I have studied in America. I watched the war in Ukraine with great interest. Every war, every battle teaches us things. We've forgotten that because every member of the PLA, PLAN, and the PLAAF assumes that what to do next will be radioed to them. Watch how the Americans fight. A young captain commands a squadron of heavy tanks. He's told there are enemy troops hiding behind a bridge. He isn't to hold to take the bridge, only that it has to be done. Look at the damn Israelis. I believe they are the best-trained and fighting force in the world. They turned Gaza into a no-man's land. They then struck at Iran, which bragged that not a single Israeli plane could breach its airspace.

"They were correct, one didn't breach their airspace, hundreds did. In the middle of a two-front war, they managed to not only defeat both enemies, but they also struck at targets in Yemen. They developed and deployed the world's first laser anti-missile system. When Iran attempted to strike Israel with hundreds of missiles, they and the Americans intercepted almost all of them. They showed the world that they might be a small country, but they are a hungry lion. The other countries in the Middle East secretly cheered for them to defeat Iran. The American anti-missile systems are much better than we thought. They have shown us their weakness. One we can easily insert into *Red Volcano*."

Xi's face darkened. "Are you saying the IDF is better than your PLA's? The people have spent trillions investing in the PLA. The people have sacrificed for almost one hundred years for the PLA."

"Sir, put them up against the Americans, and it would be a battle for the ages. They both use professional soldiers. The Americans ended the draft many years ago, the Israelis draft everyone. Everyone serves. Everyone is trained and active, or reserve members of the IDF who carry their rifles wherever they go. If I had the chance, I'd train the PLA to copy their tactics, and I'd teach them to fight how the Americans do. Once our NCOs and junior officers learn, then we'll have the world's best army."

"General, what you propose goes directly against what Chairman Mao taught us."

"Sir. I admit it is different, but if the PLA is to invade America, even if we're in place and surprise them with strikes at their bases, they will respond with thunder and lightning. It doesn't take them long to pull up their pants and go for blood, our blood. I completely agree that the only way we can beat the Americans on their home soil is by total surprise and overwhelming force. Do not forget the lesson the Japanese learned in the Second World War, behind every blade of grass in America is a rifle. Sir, according to their records, there are almost sixty million armed Americans. Millions of them are combat veterans. None of our troops have faced the face of a live enemy whose intent on killing them, and most of those fifty to sixty million can hit a person four to six hundred meters away. They are the world's largest army. They are well armed; they are the real enemy. I believe I recently read that those armed citizens own over ten million ARs and trillions of rounds of ammunition."

"General, they don't have any heavy weapons or warplanes."

"Neither did we in 1949 when we defeated the nationalists. The Ukrainians have turned the tables on Russia. They launched drones to destroy Russia's airports, and they took out most of their modern tanks. They were able to strike Moscow! What would we do if some drones found themselves striking this very building?

"The time to reorganize is before a war we could lose. I know my life is forfeit. I have lived and served the people of China for thirty-five years. I don't fear death."

"General, what do you fear?"

Jinping looked into Xi's eyes. "Sir, I fear losing."

"So do I, so here's what I want you to do. Don't waste your time writing me reports. I want you to reorganize the PLA so that when we launch *Red Volcano*, they fight like the Americans and can devise a strategy on the fly. I want them to be trained to think. I know the risk I'm taking, but I agree with you. An army that has to take orders on a daily basis from an HQ located over 10,000 miles away will lose. We can't be their all-seeing eye that knows all."

"Yes, thank you, sir. Remember, when we start, they will be watching our every move on their overhead birds."

Xi smiled. "They won't have their birds for long."

"Sir, don't believe what my counterpart in the space force tells you. It will take us almost a week to clean and reload a silo. The last time I checked, we had only one crew that passed their final exams. If we don't get better, stronger, and quicker, we'll be looking at a complete disaster."

"General, you mentioned the American Navy's weakness. What did you mean?"

Jinping smiled. "Sir, their ships only carry a small number of missiles. We can force them to use their very expensive missiles up on our drones. They have practiced reloading a few times while at sea, it took them hours to reload a single cell. If we target the support ships, they will run out of missiles and will be forced to return to one of their bases, bases we have already destroyed. Their weakness is that they thought their numbers would protect them. Only now, after watching the war in Ukraine, are they beginning to worry about the number of missiles their ships carry and the mix of missiles. Once they are run dry, we know where their bases are, we can copy the Germans' wolf pack plan and position our diesel electric boats in their path. They'll have to run our gauntlet of torpedoes. The diesel boats are almost silent when operating on their batteries.

"And of their massive carriers?"

"They will run out of fuel for their jets. Without their resupply ships, they too will be forced to return to port to resupply. I propose we target their support ships, and when they begin their at-sea refueling, we hit them with our DF 26 anti-carrier missiles. We might get lucky and strike both ships. I've studied their Ford Class and I believe I've discovered a way to neutralize them with only using one cruise missile, and it's not a nuclear weapon."

"Explain in very simple terms."

Xi listened and smiled.

Xi smiled and nodded to his general. "I approve of your addition to the plan. General, thank you for sharing your honest feelings with me."

"The others might have been thinking the same but are afraid to speak the truth."

Xi began to feel pressured, and he struggled to control his temper; he, China, needed such leaders. "What is the truth?"

"Sir, the truth is we will lose just like Japan did in the Second World War. The Americans know all they have to do is cut off our oil, and our war machine winds down. The Houthis' missiles won't know the difference between our tankers and an American ship. Our Navy will have to escort them, taking them out of the war against America.

Xi nodded. "I've been thinking of that same weakness in the plan. Can we risk some old ships?"

"Sir, where are we going to get replacement oil if they close the Red Sea? America won't sell it to us."

Xi patted the general on his left shoulder. "General, maybe we don't have to buy any oil, we'll take it from America. Once we control the key states, the oil will be ours. We could also target their oil storage site."

Jinping shook his head. "All of those ideas place our lightly armed troops against the American Army, who will be fighting on their own soil. They will be joined by their militias and armed civilians. They will fight like uncaged wild big cats."

"What are you proposing?"

"I propose we ask the troops already in America for their plan of action, if, after striking their primary targets, we have them collect the oil and then strike their secondary ones. We have to leave their major oil depots untouched."

"I see how your plan to decentralize comes into play. I will give you an answer tomorrow. Let's see if they can locate their fuel supplies. We can claim or use our strength to capture. My other thought is how could they block our ships if we hit them at the bases and mine the harbors, locking them in their damaged or destroyed by us."

"Sir, in one word. Submarines. In World War II, they were responsible for sinking almost sixty percent of Japan's oil."

Xi shook his head. "Why do you believe they can do better with our technologies?"

"They can mine the Strait of the Red Sea and the route most of our tankers take. Don't believe we can strike the Americans, and our initial attack will knock them down to their knees. The Japanese also thought the same way. The Americans were so angry that they developed the atomic bomb to punish the Japanese. I don't want to see our homes turned into radioactive dust."

Xi shook his head. "They wouldn't dare use them against us. We have atomic weapons also; if they launched, we would launch on warning."

"If they used their Trident submarines, we would have less than fifteen minutes before they struck, and their Tridents are accurate enough to be first strike missiles. Part of the plan has to be locating and destroying their missile boats. If I remember correctly, each Trident boat carries 24 missiles, each with up to ten warheads. Each boat could deliver 240 very accurate warheads."

"How many boats do they have?"

"I don't remember the exact number, I think it's fourteen, or maybe eighteen. I usually rely on Admiral Hi Kingo for information on the world's navies. He is an expert on such matters. His part of the plan must be to destroy any US Navy ships that we miss in our initial strike. He has to locate and destroy their submarines before they launch. Each of their missile boats is escorted by at least one and maybe two nuclear-powered attack submarines. I strongly suggest you read the Admiral into the plan so he can begin tracking the American missile boats and their resupply ships."

"An excellent idea. I'll contact him and will read him into the plan. I promise you I will listen to his honest opinion."

"Sir, if I may. I have one last thought on the lead up to the attack."

"I'm listening."

"We should strike one of their new carriers and make it look like the attack was carried out by someone else, someone such as the Iranians or Russians. That will force the Americans to focus on them, and they'll lose their focus on us."

"That is an excellent idea. I will add it to my discussion with Admiral Hi Kingo."

Chapter 3

The Chinese Troops Walked Into America and Were Greeted With Open Arms.

The PLA's special forces simply walked across America's southern border while the American ICE agents were busy capturing and securing housing for the thousands of Hispanics who followed the billboards in their countries offering them a new life in America. Trains carried thousands to the gate of plenty. Most simply found a border agent and surrendered themselves. This took the agents away from the border while they processed the immigrants. The PLA paid the cartels to make sure their people could cross the border and disappear.

The Chinese soldiers who got caught by the Border Patrol wore civilian clothes and spoke English, they asked for political asylum, which automatically triggered a process where they were given a ticket with the date they were to report to an immigration court, usually in five years. The soldiers couldn't believe this was how the Americans handled their border. One whispered in Mandarin, "We could have carried twenty backpack nukes into Texas, and they wouldn't have blinked."

The officer he whispered to turned and looked at the soldier. "Do you remember your training for this mission? Always speak English. Never talk in Mandarin. Never mention weapons. You are reduced to Liebing (recruit). The next time you break the rules I will kill you and bury you so deep your ancestors will never locate your soul. Do you understand me?"

"Yes, sir."

"Enough with the ranks, never call me or your officers sirs, we are civilians seeking political asylum. If their border patrol hears us saying anything else, they could kill us as spies. That's your second mistake. There won't be a third. Am I clear?"

"Yes." The officer walked toward his counterpart in the MSS. "Keep an eye and ear open to that one."

"Is he breaking the rules?"

"He is young. Let's see if he learns."

The soldier's friend whispered to him. "You almost got yourself killed. Don't screw up again. Just follow your orders and remember our training."

After getting their court ticket, they went to their prearranged pick-up location. They were pleased when they saw there were three buses waiting for them. They were met by members of the PLA and PAP who had entered the country legally a month before the troops. They had entered with the promise of creating a new company that would make electric cars. This allowed them to import a large quantity of equipment. Most of the equipment was military supplies that the troops would use in Phase 2 of the war plan. They told the border patrol agents they would be happy to hire the new Chinese and would locate them housing. The agents quickly agreed as they were already swamped with people crossing the border.

The PLA set up business in a large empty warehouse, which had been converted into an electric car factory, as their training location. The PLA commanding general of the American operation surprised his officers and the troops when he told them what their rifle of choice would be. It wasn't as many assumed, an AK or the Chinese bullpup QBZ-95; it was the American AR that could be purchased from thousands of stores, and whose ammunition was plentiful and inexpensive compared to the Chinese round, which was chambered in 5.8×42 mm caliber.

The 'owners' of the factory had been buying ARs as soon as they got their drivers' licenses. They went to gun shows and gun stores and purchased hundreds of 80% lowers that could be shipped directly to them without having to have a background check run. The other advantage the 80% lower had was that they could be milled to be fully automatic. Boxes of triggers, magazines, barrels, and other parts necessary to turn the lower into a fully functioning rifle arrived from American companies who were very pleased to handle the large orders. The commander smiled at everything he saw, the rows of brown and white delivery trucks. UPS and FedEx made daily deliveries to the factory. The commander was amazed he could order cases of ammo without the seller batting an eye. All he needed was a valid credit card.

A shiny new red Chinese electric car sat in front of the 'factory' to convince everyone they were indeed building a factory to introduce China's newest electric car to America. Their story, when interviewed by the news organizations and trade publications, was that due to the high tariffs placed on Chinese goods, they decided to build the cars in America. The governor of Texas was proud that he had secured the factory for South Texas. He bragged about the number of jobs the factory was going to create. The car was loaned to car blogs, magazines, and review sites. The car had been hand-built in China. Its suspension and batteries were copies of the Tesla Model 3 with just enough changes so they couldn't be sued for stealing their IP.

Plastic explosives, hand grenades, and RPGs were shipped to the 'factory' marked as machinery, electronic car batteries, and other parts for the cars. The CCP even shipped completed electric cars that were driven around to display them to potential customers. In China, the PLA owned many factories as a way to increase its budget. Getting into the production of electric cars was something the PLA had been handling at home, so it was easy to transfer managers to America.

A local asked the governor in an interview by the local newspaper why, if the factory was going to hire so many workers, there were so many Asian young men in the factory and why wasn't there any typical noise coming from the factory. Why weren't any local dealers contacted to carry the new cars?

The governor read the interview and stopped. He read it twice before he asked his Director of Public Safety to meet with him. He asked the director to read the interview before meeting with the governor the next morning.

The Director of Public Safety told the governor. "Sir, he's right on with all of his questions. I sent two people to inspect the factory. He could be onto something. We were so excited to win the factory, we didn't look into the background of the company. It turns out the company is owned by none other than the damned PLA."

The governor looked shocked. "The PLA? They're building electric cars?"

"Nope. I bet it's really a training facility right under our noses, and we let them almost get away with it. We approached a judge to get a search warrant, and the bad news is..."

"The bad news is, he rejected it because there's no evidence of the factory being connected to a crime. He said he even placed a deposit for one of the cars."

The governor nodded. "That's the crime. Those SOBs are using the factory to support the damn PLA. There aren't any cars being produced. The young men aren't workers, they're soldiers. We have to get eyes in the factory. There must be cameras in the building. See about hacking into their network. I don't give a damn about a warrant. Find a way to get eyes in the building."

"Sir, they could sue..."

"I don't give a damn about a lawsuit, if that is really an assembly location for the PLA we have to know their targets and timeline. Shit, for all we know they've already deployed their people right under our noses. Get the commanding officers of all of the bases in Texas on a Zoom call as quickly as you can."

"Can I tell them why?"

"No. Just tell them we stumbled on some information; they don't yet have a need to know."

"Sir, what if it turns out to be a nothing burger?"

"I can't run again, so I will end my political career as 'Chicken Little.'"

"Sir, if this blows up, your chances of being elected to anything other than a waste collector will be over."

I know it. I think we should read General West, the commander of the Texas National Guard into what we suspect."

The PLA troops trained at night so no one would get suspicious. The local police hadn't been read into what the Governor and Director of Public Safety thought. They didn't know the sharp drop in reported crime in the warehouse district was due to the Chinese electronic car company's employees who had rid the neighborhood of the local gangs. The soldiers used the gangs to keep their skills sharp.

The gangs got together, and three hundred of them attacked the electric car company's location. They were met by four hundred heavily armed and well-trained PLA soldiers who taught the gangs a lesson most never survived to appreciate. Know who your enemy is. The PLA was waiting for the gangs. Three drones had been watching their movements for weeks. The Chinese knew when the gangs were massing and when they would attack the 'factory.'

The local mayor was ecstatic about the increase in new companies that surrounded the Chinese electric car factory. The factory manager had informed the mayor that they preferred to keep their vendors close, so in the course of eight months, 85% of the empty warehouses were rented, with flocks of Chinese workers working around the clock. The police didn't know the Chinese patrolled the area, and when the local gangs arrived for their 'protection' payments, they realized too late they'd picked on the wrong people. The gang activity decreased to close to zero. Word quickly spread through the town that it wasn't a place for crime. Anyone who committed serious crimes simply disappeared. In less than six months, the crime rate dropped to almost zero.

The local police never figured out what had happened to the gangs, but they weren't complaining. They never found the bodies because the Chinese had used a backhoe to dig a mass grave where they dumped the bodies. The Chinese buried the living along with the dead. They didn't care, and the curses hurled at them by the wounded only made them smile.

While the soldiers were dealing with the gangs, the officers were reviewing the next phase of their operation. The commanding officer smiled as he read his officers their orders. "I am proud to tell you we have been tasked with two missions. You can think of the first as foreplay. We're going to wind the Americans up until they are fighting among themselves. They'll be so busy fighting with each other they won't pay attention to us as we prepare to engage them in Phase Two.

"We're going to select a city whose racial mix is heavily black and poor. We'll be setting up a situation where a white police officer shoots and kills a black man who is under the age of thirty. We'll help their media promote the killing as a racial strike against all blacks in America. The MSS has many American reporters on its payroll. They'll push the story until everyone believes the white officer targeted the black man. They will tear the heart of their cities apart for us. They will be so focused on their race problems they'll forget about us and our farms."

It should have been a simple police shooting of a looter who'd robbed a small local store. However, this time the media picked up the story that the shooting was because the victim was black, and the shooter was a white supremacist wearing a police uniform. (In reality, the police officer had fired a warning shot. It was a Chinese sniper who killed the looter with a special bullet that broke apart in the victim's body so it couldn't be matched to any specific weapon. The media, helped by the MSS's agents, published the story the MSS wanted: a white cop had killed a young black man who was surrendering before he was shot dead.)

The resulting riots against the police exploded across the country. The story was carried on every American news program. The Americans were absorbed with the story when it happened again. A white officer was said to have shot a young black male, of only fourteen, and an honor student, because he wouldn't stop when he was told to by the officer. It was a false story generated by the MSS and happily pushed by the willing media.

There wasn't a young black teen. It had all been a 'Deep Fake.' The quality of the Chinese 'deep fakes' was so good that the average person couldn't tell it wasn't real. By the time the story was proven false, the damage had already been done. Newark, NJ; Trenton, NJ; New York, NY; Atlanta, GA; St Louis, MO; Chicago, IL; Los Angeles, CA; Oakland, CA; Portland, OR; and of course, Minneapolis, MN, suffered combined damage in excess of forty billion dollars. The President had to federalize the National Guard and declare limited martial law to restore order.

Shingho decided to use the protestors to help destroy faith and trust in America and the American dollar. One of Xi's goals was to replace the dollar with the Renminbi, further weakening America and its international standing. Xi had decided there were different ways to defeat the Americans; one was to destroy their economy, replacing the dollar as the international trade currency would hurt the value of the dollar. America had a debt it could not possibly repay, one that was growing every day.

Xi held onto most of the bonds they had purchased as a sword held over America's head. If they threatened to use nuclear weapons against China, Xi would threaten to dump all of the American bonds China held, it would sink the dollar and America's economy, sending them into a deep depression that would make the one in 1935 pale in comparison.

Shingho told Xi. "Sir, my plan is that while the PLA troops in Texas are training and preparing to take a leading role in Phase 3, the riots and damage they cause will force the Americans to cut their spending on defense and other departments to repair the damage the riots caused. After the riots have ended, as winter approaches, I plan to create another incident between Thanksgiving and Christmas. The new riots will end their famous shopping season. The net result will be the failure of their largest retail stores, resulting in thousands of job losses.

"Consumer spending accounts for two-thirds of the GNP. When consumers stop spending, they will enter a depression. You can dump their bonds, but they can print money out of thin air to stabilize the price. The printing will lead to massive inflation, but it will pale in comparison to the consumers' stopping spending. Boom, America's economy will spin out of control. This time, a world war won't save them because before they can gear up to strike at us, the war will be over."

Xi told Shingho. "I like it. These riots and the economic damage they inflict will be fatal, and then we will launch our main attack and revel in watching their great experiment fail. My goal is to see our flag flying above the American flag over the White House. The foolish Americans don't understand they're allowing us to invade their country while welcoming them. If I didn't see it with my own eyes, I wouldn't have believed any of it. What other country would welcome very fit young men into their country? None. Not us. Only the green liberals of Europe and America would be so stupid as to allow our troops to just walk in. Can you imagine who else they allowed in without any vetting? They paid our troops and fed them all the while they didn't even attempt to vet them. I learned that most of our troops were given a new Apple iPhone. The Americans are crazy."

Shingho nodded. "Sir, we will stand in front of the White House when we announce that everyone in America has to learn Chinese history and our language."

Xi smiled. "A hundred years after we defeat the Americans, America will be a forgotten country, and English will be a dead language. China once ruled the known world, and soon we will again. Our history books tell the story of how America defeated itself. The lava from our *Red Volcano* will bury America and the American dream. Every other country will follow our laws, or they'll be destroyed. With America gone, the world will be ours."

In October 2026, Amazon and Walmart began delivering large numbers of drones to the Chinese factories that had spread to most states and Chinese farms. The new administration had threatened to place a huge tariff on goods made in China. Xi told the general. "I promised their president we would move many of our factories here. He never suspected that the factories were nothing but a cover. We are making drones in some of the factories, which we sell to Amazon and Walmart. They, in turn, sell them back to us without knowing who their real customer was.

No one at Amazon or Walmart questioned the large number of drones ordered by the factories and farms. The PLA soldiers worked around the clock to turn the drones into weapons of war. C4 was brought into the country in the crates with the other weapons. When the officers considered their troops sufficient in all things American, they were sent to the Chinese-owned farms that bordered America's most important military bases. Some of the PLA troops worked the fields in shifts while others prepared for the upcoming attacks.

No one reported the sound of the troops practicing on their ARs because they were all equipped with suppressors. Suppressors had been removed from the NFA (National Firearms Act) effective January 1, 2026. Orders had been placed starting in the summer of 2025 to ensure they could take delivery in January. In the states that had outlawed the purchase of bulk ammunition and suppressors, they were shipped in crates marked farm equipment. The troops held mock battles at night on the farms' fields. Models of their targets had been built and were in the barns and in the basements of the factories. The troops studied the models and repeated their orders.

Everyone was trained for the rank above and below them in case their casualties were higher than expected. The sergeants were shocked when they were told to take an objective, but not how to. They were told to develop their own plans and practice them. The NCOs took to the new orders like fish to water. They took over the training of their troops. Much to the surprise and pleasure of their officers, the NCOs were usually treating the troops fairly while they worked them harder than before.

When the calendar turned its page and the year 2027 began, Xi met with Shingho in the war bunker located four hundred feet under the People's Congress building. "Mr. President, I brought a new map showing our positions in America. We have been more successful than our wildest hopes."

"May I see it?"

"Yes, sir. I'll put it up on the large screen."

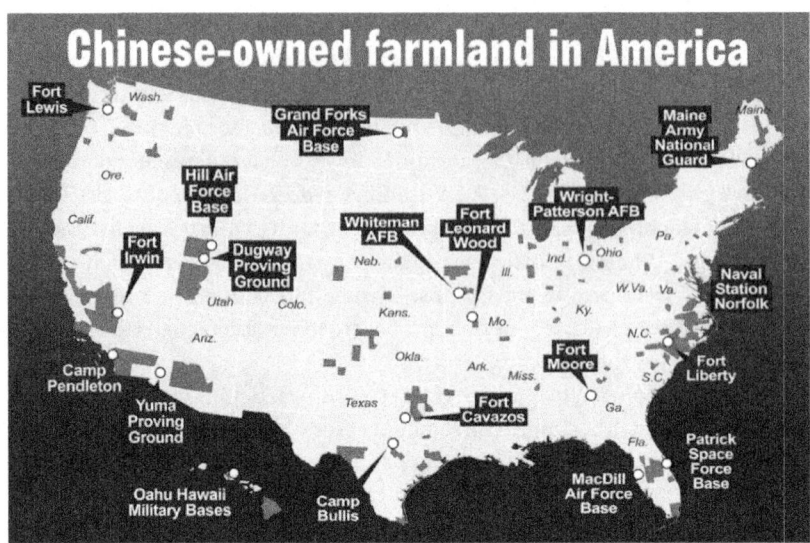

Chinese-owned farmland in America

(Please note, the map was created before President Trump's administration in June 2025 decided to change the names of the bases to what they were when Biden's Secretary of Defense changed them. For example, Fort Cavazos was and is again, Fort Hood.)

Xi studied the map. "How are the heavy weapon shipments going?"

"Sir, most of our supplies are ahead of our schedule, some are behind our worst-case projections."

Xi was getting furious. When he did, he lowered his voice into a whisper that Shingho had to strain to hear. "Can you explain why we are slowly falling further behind every day. You committed to meeting our schedule. Some of their states have passed laws prohibiting the purchase of farmland from foreign entities, and they want us to sell our existing farmland by the end of next year. They also want to inspect our farms and the factories. We can stall them long enough if we stay on our schedule. Any delays can cost us the war. Give me one reason why I shouldn't have you removed from your position and sent to a labor camp. Killing you would be too merciful."

Shingho responded. "The Americans have cut off our supply of certain materials and have clamped down on our shipments to our farms and factories. We've been informed they will begin inspecting every one of our shipments this week. They have begun to ask what our farms are doing and where the crops are being sold. They have also asked where we're selling our electric cars because, according to their state departments of motor vehicles, we haven't registered any vehicles."

Xi stood up and towered over Shingho. "Then ship them some so they can sell them and keep the Americans at bay. Tell them the crops grown are shipped here to feed our hungry."

"Yes, sir. I will see to it right away."

Xi got up and walked out of the conference room. He stopped and turned back to look at Shingho. "Fix this right now. I will not accept any more delays. I want the general in charge of *Red Volcano* in America replaced. He should have foreseen these problems and dealt with them before they set our schedule back."

"Yes, sir. I will have him reassigned."

"I didn't say I wanted him returned, I said I want him replaced."

Chapter 4
The Fruit of Deceit.

It took five years for the thousands of PLA 'immigrants' to cross the border, be trained, and be moved to the Chinese-owned farms that oversaw the key American military bases. It had taken years because the MSS and PLA didn't want any of their people captured by the American Border Patrol. They had ordered the PLA not to turn themselves into the American Border Patrol. Xi and Shingho knew that groups of young, military-aged men without families would stand out like a black eye, so they took their time in sending people across the border.

The previous American administration ran on a platform of a closed border, so the MSS and PLA began using the northern border to move their people and equipment into America. There were many areas where the border ran through dense forests, and it was easy for trained soldiers to simply cross and disappear. The new President ran on a promise to have compassion for the migrants who had no place else to go. The PRC had invested hundreds of millions to ensure the new president won and also won the House and Senate, so they could undo almost everything the previous administration had put in place.

The PLA had bribed customs agents to allow missiles and other weapons into America. The weapons had been mixed in with electric car parts, farm equipment made in China for American companies, and in sections hidden inside trucks made in China for American companies. The trucks and farm equipment stopped at one of the Chinese factories where the missiles were removed. A significant part of the war plan was for the PLA soldiers on the farms to launch an attack on the American military bases with the rockets. The Chinese company that designed and built the PLA's tanks and trucks designed a new truck that hid the launch pods under what appeared to be bales of hay. The hay bales covered a dozen 240mm rocket launch tubes.

Some of the rockets' warheads were high explosive, some were designed to spread deadly gas over their targets to knock out and kill any resistance to their attacks. Some rockets, depending on their target, were designed to destroy runways. Some of the warheads were white phosphorous (WP) to set the bases' fuel storage sites and anything else they landed on, on fire. The truck's launchers were designed to be easily pushed off the trucks and reloaded within twenty minutes. The troops practiced the reloading so they could do it in any weather, dark or light, and even if the empty launcher had caught fire. For the plan to work, speed was crucial. The troops had to destroy their targets completely and as quickly as possible to prevent a counterattack.

While most Chinese soldiers practiced firing and reloading the rockets, others were charged with defending the launch sites from any American air attack. Shipped into America, disguised as heavy-duty electric trucks, the air defense systems of the farms and factories was China's new FB10A air defense systems, mounted on Chinese 6-wheel trucks. The missile had a range of 6 miles and could intercept planes, drones, and even missiles traveling at speeds up to Mach 4.

Each farm and factory had two air defense teams, each comprised of a radar search truck and one with six launch tubes. Both were connected to the main battle room, where the radar input from all of the local facilities was merged so the commanding office for the area could decide on the best defense. In addition to the FBA10B system, each team had two soldiers with MANPADs to deal with scouts and attack helicopters.

The air defense troops practiced operating the systems in all weather conditions, at all hours. When the alarms sounded, the troops rushed from their barracks to man their systems, turning on their thermal tracking systems. They didn't turn on their radars, so they couldn't be picked up by the bases they were next to. They were only allowed to take the trucks out of the barns when there weren't any American satellites overhead or under dense cloud-filled skies. Those in the factories couldn't take the trucks out of the building because the local and state police randomly patrolled the factories. The sight of the military trucks and missiles would surely lead to a large armed response. Huge basements had been dug under the farms and factories. The basement garages had camouflaged ramps. The trucks and heavy weapons were stored in the basements so inspectors didn't see them.

While some of the troops operated the farm so that any outsider would see a working farm, the majority of the troops practiced their attack on the American bases. Many of the troops were used to dig a series of tunnels between the farm and under the bases' fences. They knew that once inside the fence line, they would pop up at the base and surprise the Americans. A secret detachment from the Third Detachment of the PLA (3PLA) arrived three months before the planned attack date/time.

The 3PLA of the People's Liberation Army Joint Staff Department was responsible for China's military computer network operations (CNO) and signals intelligence (SIGINT) operations. It has been compared to the United States' National Security Agency. They managed to hack into the networks of the bases targeted for attack.

The Chinese purchase of farmland near American bases went unreported by the Administration, which was in office from 2024 to 2028; some of the members of their federal police force (FBI) were happy to accept under-the-table donations, as were many of the local first responders. Some senators demanded donations of new cars and precious metals so the IRS and FBI watchdogs wouldn't be able to locate the donations, and the Senators wouldn't have to report them. Xi studied the number of rocket deliveries to America and shook his head. He noted the numbers showed a delta of 29% from their worst-case projections for their long-range ones.

Xi didn't accept that all the years and money spent planning to make America subservient to China were going to fail. The war plan was significantly behind schedule due to the delay of the heavy weapons. If only Shingho had acted in time and found a way to get more of the weapons to America. Xi decided it was time to change the director of the MSS. He spoke to the team leader of his bodyguard detachment. "I believe it's time for a change of leadership of the MSS. Make it look like he had a heart attack."

"Sir, his family?"

"Such a shame they died when the gas line to their house ruptured and caught fire in the middle of the night."

A smiling protection officer snapped to attention. "Yes, sir. Such a shame, at least they all died together and maybe in their sleep."

Chapter 5
Dominoes Begin to Fall.
January 2029

A significant part of the *Red Volcano* war plan was to distract Americans and split their forces so when the strike in their homeland came, they would be stretched too thin and be easier to conquer. The first domino to fall into place was the North Korean invasion of the South.

It took a huge bribe to convince Kim Jong Un to strike the South. For all of his bluster, Kim Jong Un knew his armies had outdated equipment and the only way to win was to do so before the Americans could reinforce their 20,000 troops. He wanted to kill the troops as bloody as possible, to send a message to the Americans. The North had equipped their advance troops with long, sharp knives and machetes to hack the Americans to a bloody pulp, which they would post on the internet. Xi warned Kim Jong Un not to carry out that part of his invasion plan. Xi told Kim Jong Un. "If you hack the American soldiers, they will respond with overwhelming numbers of nuclear weapons."

"We have our own nuclear weapons. We can reduce America to a barren, dead country."

Xi shook his head. "We gave you the design of your missiles. We included in the design a fail-safe' in case you decided not to follow our advice."

Kim Jong Un screamed. "Advice? You mean your orders don't, you?"

"Whatever you wish to call them. If we don't transmit a code to your missiles, they will self-explode five hundred meters above their launch location."

"We are experts in computer hacking. Of course, we knew you would attempt to control us, so I ordered our hacking department to locate your code and erase it. You do not control the People of the Democratic Korea. I have targeted Beijing, knowing you would attempt to hold us back from our destiny."

Xi smiled. He had ordered the 3PLA (Computer hacking department of the PLA) to design two sets of fail-safe controls in the warheads and boosters. One set that would be difficult to locate and remove without setting the warheads off. It was expected the North's hackers would locate the first set of codes but the second was hidden in the missiles' actual targeting software. It was buried under so much normal code that the best of 3PLA pledged to Xi the North's hackers wouldn't locate them, and if they did, they would kill themselves and along with much of the North.

Xi pretended to be worried on the call with Kim Jong Un before telling him not to launch without his permission. Kim Jong Un laughed and disconnected the call. He told his Minister of War. "He is like a spoiled child. Always getting his way. He'll either be dead soon or he'll dance to my tune. Are we still on schedule?"

The Minister knew there was only one way to respond if he wanted to see the sun set that day. "Yes, sir. All is in readiness, just waiting for your order."

The North had been digging tunnels under the DMZ for over fifty years. Some of the larger ones held a complete armor division ready to strike. Some held equipment not only under the DMZ but were already inside South Korea. The North planned to overwhelm the troops manning the border with over a thousand missiles while its armor crashed across the border. Undercover agents parachuted into the South's most important bases. Hundreds arrived in the South by submarine. Thousands were already living in the South. No one suspected they were, in reality, agents of the North working to pave the way for the North's takeover of the South.

The North's hackers began to turn the power off in the South, followed by the complete outage of phones. They even targeted hundreds of cell towers. In the dark, cold late evening, deprived of power, the Internet, and cell phones, the people of Seoul easily panicked. Many ran into the streets knowing their most feared nightmare was about to hit them. The North was coming. The South and America placed their troops manning the border on their highest alert level. The USS George Washington based in Yokosuka, Japan, recalled their crew.

The 100,000-ton displacement ship rendezvoused with the carrier's special supply ship. As it was a handful of days before the change of Presidents, the George Washington received 'special weapons' that had been removed after the Cold War by President George Bush. The Secretary of War had studied all of the available data and came to the conclusion that it was only a matter of time before China was going to strike America. He had authorized, with the President's agreement, for the return of 'special weapons' to the fleet.

Since Seoul was only 54 miles from the DMZ, the residents of Seoul knew their city would be the North's primary target when, not if, the North invaded the South in their goal of uniting all of Korea under the North's iron thumb. Many residents and store owners set alarms that, if tampered with, would set off a small block of C4 covered in BB pellets, locally made Claymore mines. They knew the North would destroy their homes and stores after the loss of some of their soldiers. The residents and store owners didn't care. They knew the North would use rockets and artillery to break the will of the South. The South also had a large inventory of surface-to-air and surface-to-surface missiles. Some were old by American military standards, but all the South wanted were missiles capable of striking the North and their advancing armies.

Seoul had thousands of shelters for its residents. Most of the shelters were connected to underground trains designed to transport millions to a safe location at the southern end of Korea. The leaders of South Korea hoped the North didn't know about the trains, or if they did, the South's military knew they would be destroyed, loaded with thousands of residents of Seoul. The South Army placed heavy machines on top of every third car in case the North attacked the trains.

Entire North Korean armies were assembled and ready to advance on Seoul. At midnight on January 18, 2029, the North Koreans struck. Three army groups popped up behind the DMZ in the South, and three attacked the troops along the DMZ. Five hundred missiles rained down on the South. Only nine and twelve of the remaining American F-16s and A-10s managed to safely take off as the North's missiles were falling on their runways and hangars. There had been a sense of hope that the North was ready to finally officially end the Korean War because just days before the attack, the North had offered to finally sign a treaty, but that hope died with the first launch of the North's missiles that were spotted by an American early warning satellite that hung 25,00 miles over the DMZ.

Many of the soldiers who typically manned their defensive positions along the DMZ were home celebrating the New Year and the hope that the war was finally going to end, and the North was finally going to announce they no longer desired to unite the two countries. As hundreds of missiles passed over the DMZ, so did two hundred thousand North Korean soldiers. Fifteen thousand of the normal 20,000 South Korean and American soldiers tried to slow the onslaught of the North.

The North sent remote vehicles into the world's densest mine field. The South and the Americans laid over twenty thousand mines along the DMZ. The drones dropped small bombs to detonate the mines. The North's tanks rolled through the clear lanes while other tanks raced out of their tunnels. While the defenders were trying to stop troops crossing the border, over ten thousand of the North's best troops burst out of the tunnels. The South Korean and American defenders were trapped between the two armies. Less than a thousand survived the trap. Three hundred managed to avoid capture by using a secret escape tunnel that brought them to a clearing three miles from the DMZ.

The South's Navy was blocked from leaving its harbors because the North had secretly mined the harbors, trapping the South's Navy. North Korean SOF soldiers left their transport submarines. A design the West didn't know existed. These were elongated old Chinese boats given to the North. Each boat carried a hundred elite troops. The submarines surfaced in the harbor, and the troops boarded inflated boats. They easily overcame the South's ill-prepared defenses.

America quickly rushed the USS John F Kennedy (JFK) and her strike group to Korea from Pearl Harbor. They were traveling at 33 knots, a speed that made their sonars unusable, so most captains turned them off until the strike group slowed, which it did every thirty minutes for three minutes, so the destroyers could use their passive sonars to check for Chinese submarines. Two Virginia-class nuclear-powered attack submarines were traveling five miles ahead of the strike group to make sure there weren't any Chinese or North Korean submarines ahead of the JFK.

They didn't know the North had layered Chinese-supplied sound-deadening tiles on their submarines, making them a black-hole in the water. Two boats were hovering in the layer while two followed the JFK from her wake, where she couldn't hear anything approaching from her stern.

The submarines had practiced their joint attack for almost a year until the orders could be carried out in the dark. When the order was finally received, the crews jumped to their feet and quietly manned their battle stations. Each boat had six torpedo tubes that were loaded with 'war-shot.' The crews entered the target data and waited for the order to fire.

The outer muzzle doors were already open, and the tubes flooded so any American submarine wouldn't hear them and attack them before they launched their attack on the American strike group. At 0230, January 20, 2029, four submarines launched a total of sixteen torpedoes and then each boat reloaded for follow-up firings. This was the first time the Russian rocket-powered torpedo had been used in anger. China purchased the rocket torpedoes from Russia, then transferred them to North Korea. Xi knew the Americans would figure out the type of weapons used and would blame the Russians.

These torpedoes couldn't turn at their high speed, so the subs had to be in perfect position to launch their 'fish' at the carrier and her escorts. The sonar operator on the USS Burke screamed into the 1MC, "FISH IN THE WATER! Bearing 180, speed 60 knots, and accelerating! ETA." He checked his computer and crossed himself. "ONE MINUTE."

The captain of the *Burke* ordered the Nixie streamed even as he knew it was useless. The North Koreans somehow managed to copy the Russian *VA-111 Shkval* torpedo that could reach speeds of 200 knots. The captain ordered a turn to head into the *Shkval*, hoping he could cut the distance down, and the torpedo wouldn't have had a chance to arm itself. He was very lucky because he was almost on top of the firing submarine, and the two *Shkvals* launched at the *Burke* hadn't had the time or distance to arm. They hadn't ignited their rocket motors yet so when they struck the *Burke's* hull, they caused two large dents and popped a handful of rivets but no real damage. The captain ordered damage control to seal the popped rivets to stop the flow of water. He then ordered the weapons officer to find the shooting sub and launch their torpedoes at it. "Weps, I want that SOB dead. Do you understand, DEAD."

"Yes, sir. I think we've got him."

"Weps, kill the SOB. No zombies, I want him so dead he'll never hurt us or anyone again."

"Yes, sir."

The *Shkval's* high speed was made possible by super cavitation, whereby a gas bubble surrounding the torpedo is created by outward deflection of water by its specially shaped nosecone and the expansion of gases from its engine and the gas generator in the nose. This minimizes water contact with the torpedo, significantly reducing drag. The *Shkval's* warhead was a high-explosive device, weighing 480 pounds. The captain of the *Burke* sent an urgent message to the *JFK*, which began to pull away from her escorts.

Her captain had ordered the reactors to 120% and kicked the massive, displacing over 100,000 tons ship to its classified top speed of over 40 knots. The Captain knew the rocket torpedoes, so he tried to turn his ship away from the course of the incoming torpedoes. In doing so, he ran right into the four fired by the two boats that had been in front of the strike force. They'd fired their torpedoes, hoping to hit one of the American ships. The carrier quickly reached its peak speed of 44 knots. She had inadvertently placed herself directly in front of the four speeding *Shkvals*.

The four *Shkvals* slammed into *JFK's* midsection. The combined 1,920 pounds of high explosive tore a sixty-foot-long hole under the waterline. The real damage was done by the next two that exploded under the ship's keel. A huge gas bubble was formed. The damaged ship was lifted up on the bubble, and then it slammed into the ocean. The keel was broken. Admiral Raymond Sticks, commander of the strike group, had broken his neck when the torpedoes struck the ship. He was knocked off his feet, and his head struck the corner of a table in his Flag bridge.

When the explosions from the *JFK* echoed through the water, the crew of the submarines cheered. It was their first and last mistake. They'd forgotten about the strike group's invisible escort, the *USS Illinois*, which had heard the launch and the cheering. The captain, Commander Karl Low, had never gotten over the nickname put on him during his Academy days, smiled. *I'm going to get our revenge on the assholes who hit my protective. We're going to show them that they made a huge mistake.*

"Captain, sonar, we've got them. Two bearing 270."

"Weps, you heard the nice lady, time you got into the fight. I want those two boats dead."

Captain Low of the *Illinois* used his light pen to mark the two boats as targets. The information was instantly sent to the four Mark 48 Mod 7 fish waiting in their launch tubes. He smiled. "Weps, silently flood tubes one through four. When ready, fire tubes one and three at the boat I've marked Sierra One, and tubes two and four target the boat I've marked Sierra Two. Reload tubes one through three with war shots and four with a decoy."

"Yes, sir. Ready to launch in fifteen seconds."

"Fire on marked bearings."

Weps looked at his board. "Sir, all Mark 48s are running hot and true. The wires are connected. Sonar is sending their updated position to our fish."

"Good. Send one to strike the boats from the port and one on their starboard side. That way, no matter which way they turn, we've got them."

Weps smiled. "Instructions sent and received by our fish. They're running in their stealth mode. They will go active when they're one hundred meters from the boats. Once they've locked in, they'll accelerate to 70 knots. Those assholes won't have any place they can go."

"They can go to Hell. Sonar, captain, watch your ears, it's going to get noisy out there."

"I'm prepared. Our fish are running hot and true. They have acquired, here they go. Hold one, this is going to be close."

The *Illinois* was rocked by the four explosions that had torn the two attacking boats apart. Each American Mark 48 carried a 650-pound warhead. The old boats were torn apart and sank with all hands. "Captain, sonar, breaking up at the two locations. We got them."

"Attention, crew of the *Illinois,* this is the captain, we've got two of them. Let's remain sharp, there may be other boats out here. We're going to show them why no one should screw around in the South End of Chicago." The crew high-fived each other and went to work silently searching for other targets.

The captain of America's newest carrier lay on the floor of the smoky CIC with two broken legs from the fall. He pulled himself to look at the damage control station. The sailor who should have manned the console lay dead. His head turned to the side from the impact with the edge of the console. He could see the flashing red lights and felt the ship being pulled apart. He knew America's mightiest warship was dying. He thought to himself, *this is all my fault when the Admiral suggested we advance at full speed, and I warned him we wouldn't hear shit at that speed. He told me he didn't believe there were any hostile boats along our path since he had us traveling north before we pushed every ship to its max. Of course, we couldn't use our max, or we'd leave our surface escorts behind us, and our attack boat wouldn't hear someone pounding on the hull. I should have told him he was wrong, and he was sending us into a potential trap. I bowed to his stars and didn't want to make waves that would block mine from happening at the next selection board. I condemned thousands and the Admiral to their deaths.*

He pulled himself into a sitting position and yelled to be given the 1MC. "This is the captain speaking, abandon ship, this is not a drill. Abandon the ship. Get as far away from the ship as you can. Get off my ship!" He looked up with tears in his eyes. His XO (Executive Officer) bent over his captain. "Sir, let me carry you to a boat."

"XO, save as many as you can and get your ass off of my ship. That's a direct order."

"Sir, what about you?"

"XO, did you not learn anything? The captain always goes down with his ship. Any word from the Admiral?"

"Sir, he's gone. Broken neck."

"Okay, the two of us will be together in Davy Jones' locker, now get off my ship and save as many as you can. XO, my final order to you is to find out who hit us and avenge our losses."

"Yes, sir. I give you my word, I won't stop until I avenge our losses."

"Thank you. Now go before it's too late. I hear her starting to break up. One little favor, can you help me into my chair?"

"Of course, this is going to hurt."

"I don't care."

The captain bit his tongue to hold back "Go while you still can."

The XO, Captain Luke Zind nodded. He felt the ship start to tilt and begin to sink. He looked at the smoke on the water from the sinking and burning escorts. "Only two destroyers left. I hope our sub can find and sink the assholes who did this."

"They will. They're the best and we're going to have our revenge."

Captain Zind slid down the stair rails to save time getting to the lowest safe place he could jump off the ship. As soon as Zind hit the water, a Chief Petty Officer helped the XO into a boat, which quickly moved away from the sinking carrier so they wouldn't be pulled down with it. The untouched destroyers *Barry* and *John Paul Jones* (*JPJ*) picked up survivors while the lightly damaged *Burke* hunted for the submarines. His sonar operator managed to get the active sonar operating. "Captain, sonar, got one. 800 yards to our portside. It's hiding in the layer."

The captain looked at his weapons officer. "Weps, can do?"

"Sir, we have four ASROCs that are responding."

"Weps, launch when you're ready. I want some revenge."

"Attention, this is WEPS, attention on the deck, attention on the deck, clear the front half of the ship. ASROCs are about to launch."

A cover on one of the vertical launch cells snapped open. A wall of flames from the ASROC engines shot up from the exhaust port. The dark gray missile slowly rose above the ship, then tipped over and headed to the location of one of the submarines. It was quickly followed by three additional rockets. The warhead of the ASROC was a Mark 54 torpedo that, once in position, was released from the rocket. A parachute slowed the torpedoes' descent into the water. It was followed by three others.

As soon as the torpedoes entered the water, they began pinging and searching for the enemy submarine that had heard the splash of the torpedoes enter the water. The four torpedoes landed in the water in a box with the attacking boat in the middle of the pinging torpedoes. The submarine had been hovering in the layer when it heard the torpedoes enter the water. The sub's captain ordered the crew to prepare for an emergency surface, hoping to avoid the torpedoes that were heading down as his boat would be zooming up.

The submarine's bow broke the surface as two of the four torpedoes chased the rising boat and struck and broke the sub's keel. The sub's captain ordered the crew to abandon the boat. It slowly slipped under the surface. Only a handful of the crew survived. Rope ladders were lowered so the survivors could climb on to the American destroyer. They were immediately taken into custody on the *Burke*. The captain was surprised when his crew pulled Northern Koreans from the ocean. The *Burke's* captain radioed the Pentagon that the survivors they'd picked up were North Koreans. He was told to keep them away from the interior of the ship. They were to be chained to the flight pad. Fed there and guarded around the clock. The captain handed the message to the XO. "Here's our orders. Make sure we pick up a few Marines who can guard them. No one is to talk to them. No one."

"Aye, aye sir. What about medical treatment?"

"XO, you never asked me that, and I'm not responding to what I didn't hear."

"Yes, sir. I understand."

"Those assholes just killed more of us than on December 7th or September 11th. The attack on Pearl sent us into World War II, which we ended by using two atomic bombs. September 11th sent us into the twenty-year war on terror. What do you think the President is going to do when he hears what just happened? They crossed the DMZ and now struck and sank our carrier."

"Sir, he's only the president for another week, do you really think he'll respond?"

The captain laughed. "Where have you been for four years? Of course, he's going to respond. I wouldn't be surprised if the B-2s or B-21s aren't already on their way."

"Nukes?"

"Depends on his mood, and since he can't run again, nothing he decides would surprise me."

"Don't you think he should wait?"

"Are you suggesting we should have waited to destroy the boats until a new president was sworn in?"

"Of course not. We had to act in order to save the lives that weren't already lost."

"I rest my case. Let's patrol the area while our brothers pick up the survivors from the *JFK*. Man, that hurts. Twelve billion just went down, with I'm guessing over two thousand hands."

"Yes, sir. I'll set a course to keep us away from the survivors."

"If you had just sunk the pride of the American Navy, where would you hide?"

"Under the survivors, where I knew the Americans wouldn't attack me."

"Right, so deploy the UUV and our tail so we can see what they can find."

With the loss of the *JFK* strike group, the decision was made to order any surviving American and Korean planes to move to Japan and operate from Japan.

The American Virginia-class boat, the *USS New Jersey*, silently searched for the enemy attack boats. "Captain, sonar, I'm holding a Kilo-class boat in layer 2,100 yards to our port bow."

"Sonar, captain, don't lose that boat."

The captain looked at his weapons officer. "Weps, your show. How do you want to spank the SOB?"

"Sir, I would swim out a Mark 48 in its slow mode and send it under the layer. Once under the Kilo, I'd turn it up to strike the SOB from its keel."

"Make it so and do it quietly so they don't know they're dead until they're in Hell."

Eight long minutes later, the last Kilo was struck by an American Mark 48. The sub was broken in half, and both sides fell into its crush zone, where they imploded. "Sonar, weps, good job. Let's increase our search area. I don't want to get caught with our pants down.

Meanwhile, in Beijing, Xi smiled, learning of the loss of the *JFK*. He looked at his Minister of Defense. "Now our plan will begin to bear fruit. The Americans will strike at North Korea, giving us an umbrella to help our ally. Next up is India and Pakistan."

Kim Jong Un learned the Americans had sent bombers to bomb us. "I want four missiles made ready to strike America." He didn't know about the hidden Chinese code that prevented Jung Un from launching his missiles without China's approval. Jong Un decided he wanted to see the missiles that would kill the Americans. He entered his launch code and smiled as the missile began to rise over its launch truck.

Once the missile reached fifty feet over the truck, the nuclear warhead exploded instantly killing Jong Un and his closest advisors. The new Korean War was going to wind down as many of the North's commanders decided to surrender to save their lives.

Chapter 6

January 15, 2029
The Next Shoe Drops, Pakistan Strikes India

On a cool January afternoon, China's Ambassador to Pakistan sat across from Pakistan's Prime Minister, Shahbaz Sharif. "I have learned that India is going to announce tomorrow they are withdrawing from the eight-decade old Indus Water Treaty. Do you have an alternative source of water? If I remember correctly, the last time India threatened to withdraw and damn the basin, you said such an act would be an act of war because it would negatively impact over 270 million Pakistanis."

Sharif placed his cooling tea on the small table between them. "May I inquire how you came to have this information?"

"Our satellites caught them working on new dams. We showed these images to their Ambassador in Beijing. Let me see, yes, it was two days ago. He confirmed that his government has decided to stop Pakistan's access to the rivers that make up the Indus basin."

Sharif pressed a button on the corner of the table that was close to his chair. The door of his office opened. An aide entered. "Sir?"

"Come." Sharif whispered something to the aide, who simply nodded and walked out of the office. A moment later, two armed guards appeared.

Sharif looked at his guest. "I am sorry to have to cut our meeting off, and I do so enjoy them. I have some issues that can't wait." The Chinese ambassador had a perfect 'poker face,' "I understand. If I or my government can be of some service, please feel free to call on me."

"I will. You can be sure I'll be in touch very soon."

The Chinese ambassador reclined in the backseat of his black Mercedes S-Class. He took a very small phone from the inside of his jacket. He looked at the slums and poor. He then pressed the autodial to a number he knew wouldn't be answered by a human. "1-9-11-0." He slid the small phone back in his pocket. He closed his eyes when the phone buzzed once. He read the message. It was one word. "Excellent."

He smiled to himself as he sipped a mug of hot tea. *We nudged the Brits to push the Indians to dam the rivers and withhold the water from Pakistan. The Brits told them what we'd scripted for them. They played their parts, the only way to conquer Pakistan without resorting to the use of WMD was to deprive them of the water that many of them require. We told the Indians the Pakistanis would strike the new dams and the army camps that protected the workers. The Pakistanis are afraid of the Indian's WMD so it will be a war that will be short and violent, one that the Indians will win, or they will believe they will win because that is the story we told them. We need them to fulfil their place in our master plan. The Indians will recoil from Pakistan's strike; they will be taken by surprise by their new weapons. The stealth planes we've loaned them, flown by our best pilots, will knock down the Indian air force, leaving them with no option except to resort to their WMD arsenal.*

The Americans will be shocked and will call for a ceasefire. They will ask the UN to intervene. The EU will agree only if America does. This will drain their resources on the eve of our main strike. I hope my counterpart in Tehran has the same success. His task will be easier than mine. The Iranians have been itching to get revenge on the Israelis since their twelve-day war in 2025. The Jews have slowed down, their last major battle with the Muslins took them six days. He laughed to himself. Six or twelve days, I wouldn't want to lead an army against the Jews. I wonder if the words in their Bible, "I will bless those who bless you, and I will curse him who curses you." I'm glad we won't be the ones attacking them.

*****

With only five days left in his term, the President was woken by his Secret Service lead agent. "Sir, the Indians and Pakistanis are at it again. This time it looks like the Indians are having their asses kicked. Sir, the Pakistanis are flying the Chinese sixth-generation stealth fighters. Indian radars are unable to track them. They're tearing the Indian Air Force a new asshole."

"Okay, I'm up. Give me a few minutes to shower and get dressed. Tell the others to meet me in the situation room."

"Yes, sir."

As the President was dressing, his Secret Service agent knocked and entered the President's bedroom. "Sir, the Iranians have launched missiles at Israel."

"The Indians and Pakistanis, Israel and Iran, North and South Korea, who's next?"

"Sir?"

"I was just thinking out loud."

When the President entered the Situation Room, everyone stood, and everyone looked tired. The wall monitors displayed the news from the war fronts. Everyone was quiet, waiting for the President to speak. "I believe we're seeing China's hands behind all of this. The North Koreans couldn't have sunk our carrier without help from either China or Russia. My gut says China is behind everything we're seeing, and I don't think they're done. My gut is telling me we're watching the coming attractions, and the main event will take place on January 20th when my replacement takes the oath. We still have time to do what's right. Order the *Lincoln* to bring her strike group home with her until we have more information about what's really going on.

The Secretary of War said. "Sir, there are reports of a large nuclear explosion in North Korea. My staff believes he tried to launch at us and the missile exploded on launch."

"Good. That's one less asshole we have to deal with. Send a message to Iran to stop now, or we will bomb them back to the Stone Age. I've had more than a stomach's full of them. We should have ended them when they took our people hostage. Pete, if they plan to strike us, what do we have to stop them, and if we can't stop them, hit them back, hit them back hard enough to shake them to their core."

The Secretary of War looked around the table and at the three Generals who sat behind him. "Sir, the *Ford*'s strike group was in the mid-Atlantic heading to Norfolk to resupply. We sent a resupply ship to replenish them mid-ocean. We've turned them around and ordered them to the eastern end of the Med. They'll be able to support Israel's defense. We learned a lot in the previous four years, we're much better prepared to handle a mass attack of drones. The *Ford* is now able to handle F-35s whose sensors can be meshed with the strike group's sensors.

"The *Reagan's* strike group is transiting the Suez Canal and will enter the Indian Ocean to support India. Sir, the Pakistanis are flying China's fifth and sixth-generation stealth fighters. We believe they are being flown by Chinese pilots. We were lucky in capturing one of the pilots talking to the others in his package. He and the others were speaking Mandarin. The *Bush* strike group was going to take up position in the South China Sea. The *Bush* is in San Diego, undergoing planned maintenance. It will take them an additional twenty months to complete the refit. The *Stennis* is in HII, undergoing its SLEP. The *Truman* just returned from a six-month deployment. We can recall their crew, resupply them, and send them back to sea. It will take some time to make ready; some minor repairs need to be completed."

The President nodded. "I think you have to find a way to speed the *Stennis* up. We're going to need every asset we can lay our hands on very soon. See if the yards can speed up the upgrades and repairs. I'd rather have a carrier strike group with a working carrier than not have a strike group. I think the *Bush* can operate without the latest radar or whatever the latest upgrades they planned. The escorts have their special radars so issue the orders. Recall the crew to every carrier in port. I learned an old saying, 'you go to war with the army you have, not the one you want.' We're going to have to fight with the ships we have."

"Yes, sir. I will look into what can be done right after this meeting. I've asked the CEO of HII to do everything they can to speed up the construction of the *Doris*

Miller. I would also like to explore what can be done to perform quick repairs and upgrades on our reserve ships."

"I thought we discussed changing its name?"

"We are looking at a list of names that will be in your hands in a couple of days."

"I like your idea of getting the reserve ships back in business. What about the battleships?"

"Sir?"

"I know there's one somewhere in Jersey and one at Pearl. They were brought back in the 80s, so why not now?"

"Sir, that's something I never thought of. I'll check with the CNO and HII to see if they can handle bringing them back."

"Good. Let me know at the end of tomorrow. What do you have in your pocket to slap the North Koreans?"

"We have a squadron of B-2s supported by the four B-21s that will destroy every one of his homes and those of his Minister of Defense. They're being escorted by six F-22s."

"If the little rocket man was close to the nuke, the war will be over very soon. Recall the planes. Let's see what happens. We can always send them if the fools keep fighting."

Pete answered. "Yes, sir. I'll have the recall code sent."

"If we have to pound them what do we have close by?"

"The *Washington* is in the Philippine Sea performing training with their navy."

"They have a real navy?"

"Sir..."

"I was joking. What else do you have?"

"Since the *Bush* is heading in the general direction, we have a day to decide. What's the status of the Golden Dome?"

"We have two test birds in orbit. Both are undertaking tests."

"Move them over the North in case they launch something, maybe the trillion we spent will be worth it. If they don't stop whatever shit the North throws at us, I hope their missile lands on the homes of the morons who sold the design to us."

"Yes, sir. I'll check with them right after the meeting. I'll also reach out to NORAD..."

"Those assholes don't worry about anything, they've got a mountain to protect them."

"Sir, they had to..."

"I know, I know. I'm just bitching. I should have seen this coming. Their timing is perfect. They pretended to agree and work with us all the while preparing to hit us. I should have remembered my Sun Tzu and his *Rules of War*. Of course, they would follow him; they were the same."

"Sir, who are you talking about, North Korea or China?"

"China. Kim Jong Un doesn't take a shit without asking Xi for permission. He wouldn't have risked attacking us without Xi's agreement. Xi wants us to strike Kim. I think I understand part of his plan. Pete, I want you to order an alert but make it quiet. No press. No leaks. Start to move our planes to their recovery airports. Put up fighters on what you call Alert 5. Arm the bombers with the nukes and get them into the air. Load a handful of B-52S with regular bombs and incendiaries. Send them to North Korea and recall the stealth bombers except for the two armed with the new bunker busters, we may need them to teach Xi a lesson he'll never forget,"

"Sir, also arm them with nukes."

"I don't want to, but yes, do it. Place our bases on alert. I don't trust those Chinese farms. I can't believe my predecessor allowed China to own land next to our largest bases and farms. Where are the crops from those farms? If there is any grown, they're being sent to China."

The President drank half a can of Diet Coke. "Tell the CNO to begin moving his ships and get them out of Norfolk, San Diego, and Pearl. If I were in Xi's shoes, those would be my first targets. The Marines can't hurt him if they can't get to the battle."

"Sir, the term is to flush the fleets."

"I don't give a shit about the right term or words, that's your job. Now go and increase security at the bases. Order the base commanders to get their Quick Response Force teams ready for anything."

The Secretary of War nodded. He wrote out a series of orders and handed his iPad to one of his staff. He whispered, put these in the proper form and code, and get them out ASAP. Declare Threatcon Delta at every base."

"Sir, every base?"

"Yes, every damn one and put the Guard on full alert."

"Yes, sir." The aide ran for the door. A Secret Service agent quickly escorted him to the secure comms room that was under the Rose Garden. "Sir, I will be right outside the door if you need anything. The room is sealed. There is an air-gapped computer you can use to compose the President's orders, which are then transmitted to the commands from the laptop under the Lexan cover."

"I admit, I've never been inside this room. The one in the Pentagon is different."

"Yes, sir. There are two techs who can help you. Both have TS/SCI clearance and are cleared to handle Presidential TS orders."

Back in the Oval Office, the President was saying. "Less than a week to go, and why now? What do the Chinese hope to accomplish? Surely they must know that when they are linked to the sinking of the *JFK*, and they will be, it will lead to all-out war between us. I want to know where and how they got those damn rocket torpedoes, China and for sure, the North didn't have them. The new president will surely want to get even with the Chinese when the truth comes out. What president would accept the loss of almost 4,000 Americans? Unless... I really hope not, but for the sake of talking, what if he knows and is helping them?"

The Secretary of War looked into the President's eyes. "Do you think he's on their payroll?"

"The one thing I've learned by being president is that anything is possible, and as long as the deep state and the media are working together, they can get away with anything. Anything. We have a week to get to the bottom of what happened and who was behind it. The media ran with the Russia BS. Don't let our alerts leak. Make you the base commanders know that. One leak and I'll bust their asses so far down they'll never be able to look up."

"Sir, do you want to go ahead with the bombing of the North? It will surely enrage China."

"The Navy is one hundred percent sure the survivors are from the North?"

"Sir, they are."

"Then hit them. Hit them as hard as we can without using a nuke."

"Yes, sir. I'll tell the B-52 pilots to continue the mission."

The bombers flew unnoticed into North Korea's airspace. Six Navy E/F-18G block 4s were a gift. Their new AI broke every radar back to where it started. As they approached their first target, four of the very new large 'bunker buster' bombs fell from the bomb bay. When the bombs reached their set altitude, their rocket engines fired, sending them down at more than twice the speed of sound.

"The new generation of bunker buster bombs had a dual mission, one to spread hundreds of sub bombs, and the second to continue down. The rocket engine accelerated the bomb to over one thousand miles per hour. It was followed by its two penetrators, whose purpose was to burrow into the roof of the shelter before its sub-kiloton nuclear weapon exploded, breaking the door's hinges open.

Each contained a hundred submunitions. Half were incendiary weapons designed to set cities and bases on fire. The other half were time-delayed anti-personnel small bombs. They were timed to explode and send hundreds of small, BB-sized, solid balls that shot out at supersonic speed. As the first responders entered the burning city, the small bombs exploded. The first responders and their vehicles were shredded. They didn't know that Jung Un was dead, and the war was being carried out on old orders.

Every government building in Pyongyang was destroyed, as were most of the workers in the buildings. Two B-21 bombers dropped cluster bombs over the troops crossing the DMZ. One B-2 dropped bunker buster bombs that destroyed the North's tunnels under the DMZ, the attack came as a surprise, the collapsed tunnels trapped and killed over 25,000 troops. Three B-52s sowed the DMZ with thousands of small land mines. The North's troops were trapped in the South or trapped trying to figure out how to cross the DMZ. The final nail in the coffin was the death of the leader of the North, along with his entire family, who had thought they were safe in a shelter under the People's Hall, where the Leader ruled. The new bunker blasters, redesigned after the strike in Iran. They had a 10,000-pound bunker buster warhead under its solid steel head that plowed into the executive shelter before it exploded.

The explosion ripped every door in the shelter open. Even the special lab doors that had created the deadly new bio-weapons. The explosions sucked the oxygen out of the shelter. Everyone in the Presidential bunker died.

5,000 US Marines landed at the southern tip of South Korea. They were joined by 10,000 American soldiers who had taken a freighter from Japan. The Marines and the Army's Special Forces led the way to meet the North's invading army. They were backed up by thousands of soldiers. The North was almost out of supplies, including ammo and clean water. Some North Korean soldiers simply surrendered, some fought to their deaths, and some ran seeking safety from the American and South Korean Armies. The Second Korean War lasted one week. Bombers and 5th-generation fighters cleared the skies of the North's planes. With the airspace cleared, the close attack planes tore through the North's armored vehicles and soldiers. The war was over when they ran out of ammo, the hungry dropped their weapons and raised their hands in surrender.

A second wave of bombers, the 75-year-old B-52s carpet-bombed all of the military bases and government buildings with fuel-air and five-hundred-pound bombs. These are the most powerful weapons, next to a nuke. The explosion utilized the oxygen in the atmosphere to fuel it, spreading a cloud of gas that exploded when ignited by small bomblets dropped from the bomb's cases. The gas mixed with the oxygen. It sucked the very oxygen out of the area. It sucked the oxygen right out of people's lungs. They created firestorms that destroyed everything in their path. Fire is a living entity. It feeds on everything in its path. Once the bombers had emptied their cargo on the North, they turned and refueled over Midway, then they flew to their recovery bases. The order not to return to their home bases was bothering the crews, but they figured if the balloon had gone up they would have heard about it and would have been directed to bases where they could be armed with nuclear weapons.

The MSS had always mistrusted the North Koreans. They supported and used them as pawns in their ongoing war with America. The North Koreans were ruled by a spoiled family who ruled like ancient kings. Their word was absolute law. Millions of their citizens were arrested for only asking for more or uttering the word, why? Now that the plan was coming to fruition, the Chinese didn't need the North, so they allowed the Americans to destroy it. Xi smiled and thought to himself, *another pawn is* removed from the board. *Very soon, the arrogant Americans are going to learn the weakness of the God they worship; technology is going to be their downfall.* The icing on the cake was when the beloved leader visited a missile silo of a missile designed in China to fly over 5,000 miles and carry a single nuclear weapon.

The North Koreans thought they had broken the Chinese code, stopping the warhead from arming.

Xi was informed by the MSS computer hackers. "Sir, they believe they have broken our codes, blocking the warheads. We knew they would find that set of codes. Nothing shows us that they've discovered our second set of codes."

Xi smiled and nodded. He thought. *"Their arrogance is going to be the weapon we use to dethrone them. Our plan is coming to a head in thirty-six hours. Their president senses what's coming but his replacement isn't so sure this isn't him just trying to remain in the center ring. We studied the Americans and their presidents, we know how they're going to react. Our plan was based on placing a new man in the White House, one we could control when our plan reaches the pinnacle. One who wouldn't jump to use WMD. It was expensive, but buying Presidents isn't like going to one of their Walmarts and asking where the aisle of available presidents is.* Xi laughed to himself. *Well, at least he's acting according to how the MSS's agents said he would.*

*****

The *Ford* crossed the Atlantic at its secret top speed of 45 knots. All of the published data on the *Ford* class said its top speed was 30 knots, which it was, if it kept her reactors under 85%. On the evening of January 19th, the Ford arrived at its ordered position and waited for its surface escorts to catch up. The submarines had no problem keeping up with the massive carrier.

Captain 'Bull' March announced to the crew. "Attention, the crew of the *Ford*, this is the captain. We can be called at any moment to launch planes to assist in the defense of Israel. We've been here and done this before. We know the score, and this time we've got new sensors and new weapons to take down incoming drones and missiles. Until our escorts catch up with us, I want our radars in their search mode. Crank up their power so we can see the air over the Med and Israel. Our destroyers with their SM3s, and 6s will be here before dawn. Until that time, we're it. I don't want to see any leakers, I want the skies clear; remember the civilians and warriors of Israel are counting on us."

March shook hands with his new CAG. Captain Paul Little. A name that didn't match the 6'6" polit was the commander of the *Ford's* air force. Little ordered two E-2Ds (Navy Air Warning planes) to be launched. One would orbit in front of the *Ford*, and one to the ship's stern

The early evening was calm with no drones or missiles that needed the *Ford* to intercept. At 0400, Captain March thought they had it made when he heard. "Radar to Captain. VAMPIRE, VAMPRIE."

"Captain to Radar, how many, bearing, and projected target."

"Radar to Capital, six flying wave top. We are the target, repeat, we're the target."

"Captain to OOD, set General Quarters, no drill. And find our surface escorts, we might need their SAM firepower."

"Weps to Captain. Engaging with RAMs, and soon they'll be in range of the CIWS."

Moments later, two of the drones turned on their tails and leveled out at 5,000 feet. "Radar to Captain, one is approaching from our stern, and the other is heading to our incoming escorts."

"Captain to bridge team, will someone please shoot the damn drones before they do something nasty."

The drone approaching the stern exploded with a flash of light. The warhead was a non-nuclear EMP generator. The pulse burned out the *Ford's* electronics. Captain March reached for the IMC as the OOD said. "Sir, all of the phones are offline. Only the sound-powered phones are working. The reactors SCRAMed, the radars just crashed and are offline as are all of our weapons sensors. The electromagnetic catapults stopped working, as did the electromagnetic arrester system. Sir, the *Ford* is dead in the water."

"Damn total electrics and electronic this and that. Someone knew exactly how to hurt our ship. We're in for some serious problems if we can't find a way to hit Control/Alt/Delete and get our systems rebooted."

His thoughts were interrupted by the outlooks, and the radar operators reported a swarm of drones five miles away with the *Ford* as their target. March looked at the OOD. "Order the Marines and anyone else who can fire a rifle and shotgun without missing a barn on the deck to try to shoot down the drones."

"Aye, sir."

"Damage control, prepare for heavy damage, and prepare to abandon ship."

LT Richard, the damage control officer, said. "Captain, abandon ship?"

"I don't see any way we can defeat those drones. If they hit someplace like our weapons lockers, we'll go up like a Roman Candle on the fourth."

Twenty-four Marines and four sailors stood on the deck and fired shotguns at the small incoming drones. They managed to take nine of them down before ten aimed at the ship's waterline, and 5 targeted the large open elevator spaces for the hangar deck that was filled with F/A-18s and F-35s. Most were fueled, and some had missiles under their wings. The drones' explosions damaged the planes, and volatile fuel leaked and caught fire. The fire caused the ordnance to explode. Shrapnel flew in all directions. Twenty crew members were attempting to control the fires. They were sliced apart by the shrapnel, as were the auto fire sprinklers and the water pipes that supplied the water to fight the fires.

The 100,000-ton ship shook from the strikes at the waterline. The nine that struck in the hangar deck caused an inferno of Hell that destroyed the hangar deck. The massive explosion tore the flight deck apart. The fires spread into other areas of the ship. Toxic black smoke filled the ship. The medics ordered everyone not fighting the fires to get to what was left of the flight deck.

Captain March looked out of the broken windows in the Flag plot. He shook his head. He knew his ship was dying. He picked up the 1MC and sighed. "Attention, attention this is the captain, abandon the ship. This is NOT a drill. Abandon the ship. Department heads report when everyone is out of their assigned stations. Damage Control, get the rafts and boats down. May God bless each and every one of you. It has been my pleasure to be your captain. We have lost all power, we have uncontrollable fires, and no way to pump the water out. We're going to sink. This is a direct order, get off my ship right now!"

The forward and rear section of the flight deck were peeled back like a peeled banana. Flames jumped out of the hangar deck like a giant bonfire. Captain March had decided he was going to go down with his ship. His XO watched the ship he loved and the captain who taught him so much what it meant to be a captain of a ship in the US Navy; they died together.

The *Churchill* was the first surface escort to reach the *Ford*. She ran into the drones looking for the surface escorts. Six drones struck the destroyer that was racing to the *Ford* at 34 knots. The first drone struck the forward vertical launch cells. The explosion and fires set off the thirty-six missiles in the cells. The explosion tore the bow to the front structure. Water rushed into the boat as five additional drones struck her. One penetrated the helicopter hangar. Its explosion caused the fully fueled helicopter to explode. The explosion reached the decks below the hangar. One was filled with helicopter-delivered ordnance. The explosion and shockwaves cut the ship apart. The stern, up to the front structure, quickly slid under the waves. The middle section, powerless and barely floating, was struck by two additional drones. It leaned to its Port side and slipped under the water.

"Mr. President, we just lost the *Ford* and the *Churchill* to a drone attack."

"How the hell did some drones know how to take out our carrier? I thought those things were unsinkable."

"Mr. President, anything that floats can be sunk."

"Shit. Do you know who and how they accomplished it?"

"Sir, the initial attack seems to have been an EMP attack that knocked out everything on the ship, allowing the next wave to strike the *Ford*. She was defenseless and took at least fifteen hits. Some of the Marines shot down some of the drones with shotguns. We lost almost 4,000 people when the *Ford* went down, and another 300 when the *Churchill* went down. We believe the weapons were Chinese that were launched by the Houthis."

"How much time do we have before the transfer of power?"

"Sir, five hours."

In Beijing, the mood was one of celebration. The PLA had launched the drones at the *Ford* from bases in Yemen. They had modified hundreds of drones made in Iran and shipped to Yemen. The PLA had told the leader of the Houthis that they could show them how to sink the American warships.

When the CIA reviewed the debris of the shot-down drones, all of the evidence pointed to Iran. The President was so informed as he was climbing into the armored beast that would take him to the swearing-in of his replacement. He felt his replacement, being Jewish, would hit the Houthis very hard. He wasn't so sure he would make China, whom he felt in his gut was responsible for the attack, because he had been briefed by the CIA, Iran didn't have the technology to produce small EMP warheads that could fit into their small drones. He told his Secretary of War. "I know the Chinese were behind the attack, but I don't understand what they hope to gain. Surely, they knew we would learn the truth, and when we did, we'd unleash hell on them."

Chapter 7
The New Pearl Harbor. Part 1.

The man who placed his hand on the Bible had been a long shot when the primaries began. He was able to outspend all of his opponents combined. Hundreds of millions had flowed into his campaign from the electric vehicle industry because he promised to put new incentives for the purchase/leases of EVs He had been a governor of his state in the Midwest, and he was Jewish. He would be the country's first Jewish president. He won the primaries by moving his party to the center and successfully won a very narrow victory over the man who had been the Secretary of State for the previous four years. The current president attempted to reach the president-to-be on the phone to warn him of what his staff had suspected. The soon-to-be president had given his cell phone to his CoS with orders not to disturb him, unless aliens invaded. The new Vice President was known for her massive social network presence. She had been in Congress for only three terms of two years each. She had been selected in order to appeal to the far left of the Party, who had once owned most of the slaves in the country.

The CoS to the new President had turned his phones off, so they never received the warnings from the previous president, who told his team, "We'll do whatever we can to support him, he doesn't have a team in place yet. We, the country, can't wait for him to pull one together. I want each of you to offer any assistance you can. If he says, no thanks, then at least we tried."

The Secretary of War asked. "Mr. President, what should we do if they turn our offers down?"

"Go home and take shelter and prepare for a war on our soil."

"Sir, you're still president until he takes the oat..."

"I understand where you're going. Let's help our new President a little. Let's make sure we're prepared for what my gut is telling me is coming. Mr. Secretary, set DEFCON 2."

The Secretary of War smiled. He pulled his encrypted phone out and sent a text to the War Room under the Pentagon. As soon as the text was received, the well-rehearsed staff went to work. Alerts were sent to every American base around the world. All were ordered to seal their bases except to allow their people back in. All leaves were cancelled. The Air Force began the process of arming the B-52s, B-2s, and B-21s with nuclear weapons.

Bombers and refueling planes were scrambled to their fail-safe locations. Fighters were scrambled to fly CAP (combat air patrol) over the country. The FAA issued a NOTAM stating that the airspace over the US was being closed in fifteen minutes. There would be no commercial or private takeoffs. Planes that couldn't make it to their destinations were ordered to seek another runway. Passengers were to remain on the planes until they were cleared by the TSA and members of the DHS.

DEFCON 2 set off a series of motions. The Joint Chiefs had their phones turned off, so they didn't get the warning. Almost no one at the ceremony had any idea the country would be under attack in a matter of minutes.

Most of America's soldiers, Marines, sailors, and airmen had returned toward the end of the first week of January. The base commanders/ship captains were informed of the change of the country's DEFCON status. A few of their aides asked if this was something that happened whenever a president was sworn in. "No. Set the alarm. Start the clock, and let's get ready for anything—issue live ammo. Increase the rapid response teams." The 82nd Airborne and the 101st grabbed their go-packs, then they waited on the taxiway aprons for their C-17s. Navy ships were prepared to leave port even if they didn't have their entire crew. Radars were engaged, and the skies and seas were scanned for threats.

Commercial flights approaching the coasts of America quicky had fighters checking them over. Pilots who'd been pilots in the Air Force or Navy realized the fighters were armed with live air-to-air missiles. This wasn't a time to play games. They spoke to the fighter pilots on Guard. They were asked to confirm their identity, their flight number, and their flight plan. They were told that if they didn't answer correctly, they would be fired upon.

Thousands of troops were watching the new president being sworn in when the alarms on their bases began screaming. They had practiced responding to the alarms to the point that it had become muscle memory. They responded as second nature. The sounding of DEFCON 2 in the minutes before the president could repeat after the Chief Justice saved thousands when the attacks began.

As soon as the new president was sworn in, the previous President was boarding his own plane. He had told the new president he preferred his plane, plus it had been updated at Boeing for a whole year with a new communications package and decoys, chaff, IR decoys, radar jammers, and in-air refueling. He told his pilot to head toward the North Atlantic. He feared his houses would be a target, so he wanted to wait until the dust settled before he decided where he and his family were going to sit out the attacks. His wife, two sons, their spouses, and his grandchildren sat in the lush leather seats, wondering what was wrong. His youngest son figured it out. He told his brothers, "I believe we're under attack and Dad wants to keep us safe, so we're going to be taking some laps up and down the East Coast."

His eldest son asked, "Isn't there anything we can do to help them?"

His youngest son looked out of the window to see two F-22s escorting the large Boeing 757-2J4 ER. His plane only carried sixty people in large, business/first-class-type seats that reclined, allowing passengers to catch some shut-eye on the flights. Today, it carried only twenty people. His family, four of his closest advisers, and, of course, the ex-President, and four Secret Service agents. The plane also had an office, conference room, and bedroom. The plane with a full load of passengers could fly 7,500 miles after Boeing had added two additional fuel tanks to carry more fuel. There was also a special luggage compartment that was designed to hold various weapons. The Secret Service changed the magazines in their weapons with special rounds designed not to puncture the plane's skin.

As the governor took the oath of office, all hell broke out across the country. One of the aides to the Chairman of the Joint Chiefs tapped the general on his left shoulder. "Sir, look toward Arlington, doesn't that look like a plane is falling out of the sky?"

The general turned to look. "I don't see anything."

"Look at your two o'clock."

The Pentagon was full of people running back and forth with reports of the attacks when an unmarked Boeing 777-300ER that was fully fueled and loaded with twenty-five thousand pounds of high explosives dove from thirty thousand feet nose first into the Pentagon's courtyard. The pilot had been given the choice of flying the plane into the Pentagon and knowing his family would be taken care of for three generations, or he could watch as they were slowly tortured to death. The pilot silently prayed to his ancestors to keep an eye on his family as his plane smashed into the center court of the Pentagon, as the new president said, "I do." The plane with fuel and explosives weighed over 540,000 pounds. It was traveling at 675mph when it struck the ground. The explosion dug a hole seventy feet deep. The shock wave cracked the war bunker under the central green zone. The shock wave also blew out four of the rings of the Pentagon. Thousands were killed in the explosion and the resulting fires that destroyed the remains of the Pentagon. The fires from the burning fuel flowed like burning ocean waves.

Windows were shattered within a five-mile radius. The blast waves struck the bridges on Highway 66 in front of the Pentagon, which collapsed, killing everyone on or under them. A second plane struck the Capitol Building while a third struck the White House. All three planes were on approved flight paths, and all had declared an in-flight emergency and requested the shortest and quickest route to Reagan International Airport. All had ignored the message that the airspace over the country was closed. None of the three had escorts, so they were free to continue on their suicidal missions. It was a freak event that wasn't held at the Capitol. The construction and repairs were a month behind schedule. The construction company had discovered black mold that had to be cared for before they could complete the repairs, so the swearing was held on the Mall in front of the Washington Monument. The delay saved the lives of over a thousand people.

The Chairman of the Joint Chiefs said. "Shit. I see it. Unless I'm wrong, it's going to strike the Pentagon. Send a full alert, move us to DEFCON 2."

The aide replied. "Sir, I turned my phone on to take some pictures of the plane when it beeped with the message the previous president used his authority while he still had it to move us to DEFCON 2. His message also said we've lost the *JFK*."

"I should have known the previous president would have his hands on the potential of a terrorist strike. I want confirmation from every base, now set Threatcon Delta, no drill. Tell the CNO I suggest he flush every ship that can move, get them out of their docks, which makes them a perfect target. Find out the real status of the *JFK*."

"Sir, my phone is full of texts. The CNO said he was already in the process of getting his ships out of their docks. The boss of the AF strike command said he is following direct orders from the previous President and has been loading nukes and sending his bombers to their fail-safe positions, and is sending fueling planes up as quickly as he can get them fueled. Make sure the Secret Service knows and gets the President out of here ASAP. I don't like having all of us sitting in one place. We're making ourselves a damn sitting duck target. We're going to get out of here right now."

"Tell him to get the planes off the ground. If this passes, he can always add fuel, but if this expands into a full war, he's going to lose his bases and his fuel."

"Yes, sir."

The chiefs saw the horizon light up from the explosion of the plane crashing into the Pentagon. The general nodded. "Get my car."

The general tapped the Commandant of the Marines. "Did you see that?"

"I did. I was just about to tap you. We're under attack."

"I shouldn't have to ask, but your Marines?"

"I placed us on Threatcon Delta before you ordered it. My Marines are itching for new orders. I received texts from all of our bases, they're all on full alert. Our on-water corps are also ready to respond to any orders. Our rapid response teams have been tripled, and they are patrolling from inside and outside of our fences. My real concern is the Chinese-owned farms that are too damned close to our bases. They should never have been allowed to own land that close to sensitive areas."

The Chairman nodded his head. "We've got to get out of here, and looking at the smoke rising over Arlington, I'd say we need a new place to coordinate this battle. The first on CONUS since 1812."

They were shocked when the Capitol Building exploded after a second plane struck it. The General nodded to his aide, "It's time we move to Site R. Bring the others and send the change to place us at DEFCON 1 status. Send an urgent message to the President's Secret Service team, instructing them to evacuate the President immediately and proceed to Site R. I have Marine One on its way to pick the President up; it will be escorted by three AH-64 helicopters. They are due in three minutes."

His aide nodded. "Sir, DEFCON 1? WAR?"

"I know. We've never been at one since we began using it in the Cold War. Those attacks on the Capitol and the Pentagon are the first of many I feel that we are going to have to deal with. This is a direct order, move us to DEFCON 1!"

"Yes, sir. I'll send it right now."

The Secret Service was alerted to the threat of over one hundred suicide drones heading to their location. ETA five minutes. They waited until the President was formally sworn in before they dragged him off the stage and into the 'Beast,' his armor-plated car that was taking him to Marine One, which was landing on a section of the road closed by the D.C. Police and the Secret Service.

When the governor removed his hand from the Bible, the Chinese troops hidden in the farms and factories fired mortars and rockets at America's military bases. The new President was pushed into Marine One, which flew a few feet above the ground. One AH-64 flew in front of the President, and one flew on each side of him. Just as Chinese missiles landed at Joint Base Andrews, where Air Force One was waiting, six F-22s and six F-15EXs were able to get airborne. One missile scored a perfect bullseye on Marine One as it was touching down. The helicopter exploded into thousands of burning pieces, including the new President.

The last F-15 pilot to take off reported to the other eleven planes. "Marine One is gone, repeat, the President is gone. No one could have survived that. The missile struck it as if it was about to touch down. Whomever is behind this is close. Those drones and rockets are short-range, maybe only twenty miles. Three rockets struck

AF-One. It's a total loss. I suggest the VP, I mean the President, be taken directly to Site R. Get her as far from this madness as possible."

The pilot of the first and squadron leader of the F-22s, Colonel Jason Rings, call sign 'Diamonds,' reported. "The Pentagon and the Capitol are gone. The plane that struck them must have been loaded with fuel and bombs because whatever is left, and it's not much, is burning."

The pilot of the third F-22, Captain Mary Nobel, was flying in circles over Washington, reported. "The ruins of the White House are burning out of control. I can't see any parts of a plane that might have hit it. Maybe more of those suicide drones or rockets."

Diamonds shook his head. "They scored with the White House, Capitol, Andrews, and, according to my messages from First Base, an AWACS, Camp David is burning out of control. I-95 is jammed, bumper to bumper, large crash of two trucks and six cars. State Police believe it was staged. One of the trucks is a propane truck, and the other is carrying gasoline. When they blow, there won't be anything left of 95 South in that area. The blast is going to leave a huge crater and kill everyone in their cars, hoping someone clears the crash."

Diamonds silently nodded. "It has to be the Chinese. I bet they moved on Taiwan at the same time they hit us. Look alive out there, I don't believe their bombers are here. Remember, they have stealth bombers. Keep your eyes open. To be safe, Raptors three and four increase the size of your circle. Eagles three and four, check out Baltimore and Annapolis. Everyone, we may be the only fighters up here. I'll see if I can find us some fuel."

Diamonds reported. "I've just received an update. The VP is being sworn in on a new Marine One which is a regular bird. Eagles one and two take up an escort role of her bird, after you check out the area around Site R. It would be like them to be waiting at Site R for the President. It looks like they got the timing down pat on the rest of this mess."

"WILCO." The two F-15s turned and headed south at Mach 2.2. They arrived over the site and the pilot of Eagle One, Captain Eileen Willis, reported. "Sir, it looks like WW 4 started down there. There must be a thousand armed assholes trying to get past the Secret Service and Marine Sentries to get into Site R. The guards are returning fire with live ammo, and the armed assholes are shooting the guards. From here it looks like the attackers are winning."

Diamonds shook his head. "Do you have anything to break up the crowds?"

Willis nodded to herself. "Sir, we left with whatever they threw on us. Twenty-Mike-Mike is in the green. Have five-zero-zero rounds and two APKWS (Advanced Precision Kill Weapon System). My partner has the same."

Diamonds smiled. "Excellent. Please deliver the mail to the crowds below and try not to hit the good guys."

Willis and her wingman turned to place them in the perfect position to launch their rockets and not strike the good guys. They lined up and fired a total of twenty-eight 2 ½ inch missiles into the crowd. The rockets had been designed to launch and wait for drones to enter the perfect launch window or target a ground target. The pilot or the weapon's officer could select the target. The second round of 14 missiles followed the first. They were centered on the crowd forming in the parking lot. The two planes pulled up and headed nose down at the crowd, and then their 20mm cannons opened fire. Both planes were out of ammo in less than ten seconds.

The 20mm rounds turned a human into a bloody mess. The speed and impact of the rounds would usually go right through a protester and kill the one behind the one who had been struck first. The Eagles began to come around and hit them again when more cruise missiles, fired from a Frigate offshore that had been on a training mission when they received the warning order, were fired. They had been listening to the Air Force's radio traffic between the F-22s and F-15s when the captain of his small crew decided to launch his cruise missiles to take out the protestors who were shooting at the Secret Service and Marines.

The cruise missiles dropped hundreds of small claymore-like devices that spread BB-sized pellets at over 600mph over the crowd. Between the fighter-launched missiles and the cruise missiles, the protestors stopped and fled for safety from the death from the sky. No one knew for a fact who was attacking them, but they knew the country was under attack.

The Vice President had just been sworn into office. She sat silently in shock, not believing the country was under attack and the President was dead. As soon as the helicopter landed, she was grabbed by the Secret Service and pushed into an Army M1 main battle tank that was surrounded by two hundred police and Sheriff deputies from both Virginia and Maryland. She screamed she needed to be at the White House. She tried to order the tank commander to take her back. He refused, telling her the country was under attack.

"It must be those damn white supremacists, it's time we put an end to them once and for all."

The tank commander shook his head. "It's not white supremacists, we believe it's the Chinese."

She laughed. "The Chinese wouldn't attack us. They know we're going to undo the tariffs and taxes the president, who should be arrested for abusing his power, put on them. Now take me to the White House."

"Ma'am, there isn't any White House, nor is there a Capitol Building or Pentagon."

"I don't believe you."

The tank commander showed her his phone, "Look at the pictures. Still believe your yellow buddies wouldn't attack us? Look at the flag on the rudder of the plane that struck the Pentagon."

"That's something you painted on the plane. The military didn't want us to win. You refused to support our platform of extending a hand to the Chinese."

"Like your party did on 9/11 or on December 7th? Words only work to their benefit. This isn't the time to talk, it's the time to fight back. As the previous president once said, 'Fight, Fight, Fight."

"Please, this isn't the time to play who's bigger. The Chinese are our friends. These simple attacks were most likely carried out by people like you."

The two Eagles flew over the CIA's headquarters and reported that it had been struck by at least six rockets. They were ordered to check on Dulles International Airport. The Eagles reported the runways had been struck with rockets that burrowed into the thick concrete and exploded, creating large craters, making it impossible for planes to land or take off. They also reported that the control tower had been struck, and the upper section where the air controllers worked had been ripped off from the tower. They reported two rockets just striking the fuel farm, which exploded in a bright flash with flames that shot up over one hundred feet. The 12 planes were ordered to land at the Marine Corps Air Facility Quantico, located in Quantico, Virginia.

The Chinese didn't know they had killed the president. Nor did they believe the story that most Americans were armed and would fight the Chinese troops when they showed themselves. They had gamed the attacks and after actions based on the profile the MSS had assembled of the new President. Their next moves were taken to protect them from an American nuclear strike.

The Chinese knew they had a very small window to secure the Americans' Minuteman missiles. China had converted one of their newest silos to, as closely as they could, what an American Minuteman silo was. They went so far as to copy the formula of the concrete used in the construction of the silos. The Chinese spent months attempting to destroy the silos without using nuclear weapons.

Another team practiced shooting down a Minuteman missile as it left or very shortly afterward. It rose over its silo. Different methods were used to simulate blocking the missiles. After four months constructing a copy of the American silo, the Chinese decided they couldn't ensure their rockets could break through the cover, and if they blew up the tracks the cover slid on, the Americans could detonate an upward-facing high explosive to blow the cover away from the silo. If that option was selected, a heavy steel mesh automatically covered the missile to protect it from any shrapnel from the covers, which couldn't damage the missile.

They also learned that saying a MANPAD could bring down an ICBM was different in theory than actually doing it. The Minuteman missiles were 'hot' launched. The extremely hot exhaust kept the shooters too far away, and while the small missiles could and did lock onto the heat of the missile's exhaust, the reality of actually hitting a rapidly rising missile was proven to be almost impossible. This meant the Chinese had to find a way to disable the missiles from being launched.

The Chinese modeled different solutions, five different teams were assigned to the same problem, all came up with the same suggestion of parking a very heavy truck on the silo covers and a second truck filled with concrete or anything else very heavy were to be set on the tracks next to the cover so even if it could slide back, the second truck would stop it, thus stopping the launch. When asked about the Americans' plan to blow the covers off if they didn't move, one of the teams said. "Good, then our team on site can toss explosive backpacks down the mouth of the silo. These will make holes in the mesh, and our follow-up tosses will break through and explode next to the missiles. The missile will be knocked off of its base, and if it could fly, it would run right into the concrete walls and explode." When the President took his oath of office, the Chinese gave the order for the trucks to break through the thin chain-link fences and park on and next to the silo covers.

As the trucks were parked on the silos, helicopters landed in front of the 'house' that was above the launch capsule. Two teams of Chinese special forces troops traced the fiber cables that carried the launch orders to the capsules. The other team, wearing Air Force uniforms. entered the houses and sprayed automatic fire from small HK5 submachine guns. The JHP bullets tore through the Air Force personnel who were trying to reach their self-defense weapons. The last thought of Captain Brian Mays was, *Why? Where was the warning?*

He died as their radios began screaming out a warning, and the nation was declaring DEFCON 2, then, less than fifteen minutes later, had they been alive, they would have been shocked when their DEFCON lights, mounted on every desk, turned red, strobing, meaning America was at WAR. Only a small handful of people survived because the Chinese misunderstood the distances, from their hide locations to the silo controlling 'house.' The Chinese also learned not to ever pass a school bus when it was loading or unloading students. Many of the schools had closed at midday so their students could watch the ceremony with their families. State Police stopped the Chinese rushing to six groups of silos. At first, the officers thought they had stumbled onto some kind of human trafficking when an officer asked to speak with the officer outside of the truck. He expected the Chinese to offer him a bribe that would add to the charges. The officer thought about what he was going to need to transport them to his station.

"You can exit, come out of the truck with your hands over your head. If I see a weapon, you'll be a dead whatever."

The officers had been told the local police were easy targets to accept a bribe so the Chinese officer exited the truck and asked permission to lower his hands so he could show the police officer his ID.

"Slowly and make no sudden moves."

The Chinese handed the officer a leather folder containing his ID, which had five one-hundred-dollar bills wrapped around the license. The Chinese smiled. "Are we good to leave?"

"Yes. If you wait one moment, my backup will be here to escort you."

The Chinese thought this was better than he could have hoped the stop would turn out.

Just before the Chinese could respond, three state police cars roared to a stop. The passengers jumped out holding a 12-gauge pump shotgun. The officer who stopped the trucks smiled. "Now that we're all here, let's get everyone out of your trucks." The Chinese officer said something in Mandarin. Moments later, everyone in the trucks stuck a gun out and opened fire on the state police officers, who had been taken by complete surprise.

The Chinese officer kicked the police officer who had stopped them. The officer didn't move. He was dead like the other six. The Chinese had three automatic weapons that tore into the police cars. The Chinese spit on the dead body and told the ones in the trucks to push the bodies into a gully next to the road. He then tossed a thermobaric grenade into the four State Police cars. He yelled. "Hurry, time is running out."

The Chinese knew that without the launch codes that released the PAL locks on the warheads, the missiles' warheads couldn't explode. The Chinese spy in the Pentagon had supplied them with the locations of the newly laid fiber cables. They used a modified chainsaw to cut through the metal pipes that carried the fiber cables. The Chinese knew they couldn't succeed in a frontal attack on the launch capsules, so they planned on cutting them off from being able to communicate with the Pentagon, the White House, and the other launch capsules. In order to get the launch officers to surrender and give the Chinese the launch keys, they planned to drop gas grenades into the vents that were hidden above ground. In an all-out nuclear war, the launch officers could close the vents. They had bottled air to keep them going for five days.

The launch officers thought something had happened to their air supply, and since they hadn't received a launch order, they could leave the capsule and call for help from the house. They could switch to their reserve air they would use in a nuclear attack to keep fallout out of their bunker.

The Chinese were waiting for the Americans to surface. They knew the layout of the house and where the tunnel to the launch capsule was located, so when the hatch opened, the American launch crews were met by hand grenades and automatic weapons that poured almost fifty rounds into the two Americans. Once they were killed, the Chinese put on scuba air tanks and stripped the launch capsules of their computers and the notebooks that contained the Americans' SOP for launching their

Minutemen missiles. After the silos were stripped of their secrets, the Chinese placed plastic explosives in the capsules to destroy them.

The Chinese believed they would have plenty of time to remove the missiles and learn any secrets the missiles had. What the Chinese had not placed in their formulas were the large numbers of armed citizens, many of whom were recent vets from America's twenty-year war against terror. Four Chinese attempts to move the trucks and gain access to the missiles failed, and the PLA troops were driven back from the mass of gunfire from the armed citizens. Even the PLA's helicopters were shot up and would never fly again unless new engines and the cockpit were replaced. The engines were shot out, and the interior of the bird was covered in blood and what the Chinese thought were shot up and useless controls.

The local Chinese who had communicated with the embassy, which kept Beijing up-to-date, were confused since the ground commander of the ground campaign was cheerful and very respectful to their leader. The Chinese found themselves in a deadly crossfire with the American military behind the fences and the American hunters and regular armed citizens in the woods outside the fenced-in restricted area. The American hunters used large hunting guns designed to bring game animals down; these knocked down any human they managed to hit, and their aim was perfect, honed by years of hunting. The American hunters searched and made the officers and NCOs their first targets. The PLA troops were left without leadership. When they realized they were leaderless, many threw their weapons down and raised their hands. The armed citizens told the Chinese to F-off and killed every member of the PLA. The Air Force NCO who was in command of the airmen behind the fence said. "Listen up. I'm in charge of the defense of this silo. I appreciate all the help. Let's see if we can dig some foxholes to help us better protect the silo."

The citizens laughed. "We don't have the shovels, do you have any? Guns and ammo we have. Shovels we don't have. We want the heads of the assholes who invaded our country; they deserve to die, and we'll continue killing them wherever we find them."

"Good, let me help you. I'll get the shovels. We have enough mags and ammo, we can give you some."

The leader of the American armed citizens walked out of the woods while carrying an AR slung over his chest and wearing body armor. He also had a semi-automatic sidearm in a holster mounted to his armored vest. "We would most likely give you some. I say we find and kill every damn commie we find. Our next stop is the farm a klick that way." He pointed over his left shoulder. We saw their smoke trails, one of us drove past their farm, and saw them launching rockets from the back of trucks. We're guessing their rockets were aimed for the Air Force Base that hosts B-52s. We're going over there to clean that Chinese nest. I'll leave some people to help guard this silo, and others.. Do you want to join us in kicking some Chinese ass?"

"I have to stay and guard the silos."

"I understand. Want a radio to stay in communication with us?"

"Thank you."

"I'll call if they try to get inside the silo." The NCO spent a minute thinking, then he nodded. "I'll bring half of my people and leave the other half here in case some are hiding and will try to hit us again. Your people will help us a lot. I can use them to guard some of the other silos I'm sure are under attack."

The American, Walter Leggings shook his head when they approached the base and saw two B-52s burning and smoke rising from the fuel farm. "God-Da— Chinese. We should have stopped them back in 49 when they were fighting for nationalists for control of China. Everyone, stay awake. I want one squad to be with the medics as they check the wounded, and everyone else break into your squads and check the base. Look inside every room and tear the place apart. Don't kill any of their officers. I want to question them."

One of the squad leaders, Sergeant Phil Outings, nodded. "Can we kill any of the Chinese we find? Can we kill them anyway we want?"

"What do you have in mind?"

"I see a lot of trees. Trees mean wood, wood means we can make crosses and crucify them."

Leggings looked at the Air Force NCO, "You have a military radio, I think you should check in and see how bad we've been hit."

"Good idea. Were you in the military?"

"Marines. Fought in Gulf War One. Twenty-three years and out. I run a small fishing and hunting store."

"That explains a lot."

"I've got a really bad feeling about this. I think this is just the beginning. Stay sharp."

"I do too."

"Check in with the Puzzle Palace to see what they know."

His cell buzzed. "What they know is DEFCON 1."

"Oh, holy shit! We're at war with China. A real mother of a war. We'd better get those silos ready. I think we're going to need them real soon. There's going to be fireworks   tonight."

Chapter 8
The New Pearl Harbor Part 2

The Chinese had managed to smuggle thousands of segments that can be assembled to produce thousands of rockets. They arrived in crates labeled as farm equipment for their farms, as well as other crates marked as components for the electric car factories. Bribes were paid to keep the customs inspection teams away from the crates and trailers loaded with the crates. The missiles were sent to the farms that were close to the key bases, such as the US Navy base at Norfolk, Virginia, and the farms close to Fort Hood, Fort Bragg, and the Marine Corps bases at Pendleton, Quantico, and the Marine Corps Air Station Cherry Point. The Chinese knew the only way they could win was to wound the American military so badly it wouldn't be able to respond and would sue for a cease-fire.

The Naval base at Norfolk, which is home to the world's largest naval base, received enough notice of the attack for them to flush most of the ships before the Chinese-owned farm less than five miles away that managed to launch their first hundred missiles. The ships had received the order to "EMERGENCY STORIE" (leave port right now) and the DEFCON 2 alert. Eighteen Burke-class destroyers managed to escape. The one nuclear carrier, the USS John C. Stennis, CVN 74, that was at the HII facility couldn't generate enough steam in its reactors that had been shut down for maintenance in time to leave before the Chinese missiles arrived.

Two small missiles struck the thousand-foot-long flight deck, two overshot the carrier and landed in the harbor. The fires were quickly put out when the captain ordered the wash-down system turned on. Water was pumped from the harbor and discharged through high-pressure nozzles covering the flight deck. The system was designed to wash nuclear fallout off the deck in case of a nuclear war. The fires had spread to the hangar deck, but with the blast doors closed and no planes on the carrier, the fires were contained by the overhead sprinkler system.

As the missiles continued to rain down on the base, the Stennis managed to shoot down six missiles with her RAM missiles and one with her close-in self-defense 20mm cannon that used a radar to track its target and a second radar to track its bullets. This enabled the gun to adjust its aim. The Stennis' air wing had been at the Naval Air Station Oceana and took to the air when the DEFCON alert sounded. Some took off without weapons, but the crews had saved the valuable planes. They were very lucky that among them were two E-2D AWACs and two refueling unmanned drones.

The E-2Ds began feeding information to the airwing, where the incoming drones and rockets had been launched from, and their bearings, so the fighters could shoot them down. America had been very slow in learning the lessons of Ukraine and the war between Hamas and Israel, where one of the main weapons were small suicide drones. The Stennis' air wing was armed with air-to-air missiles and its regular 20mm cannons. None were armed with the new laser-guided 70mm Advanced Precision Kill Weapon System II (APKWS II), which was designed to intercept drones, or the 240mm rockets used by the PLA.

The planes watched the missiles strike the base and HII's massive buildings. Most of the assembly and manufacturing buildings were undamaged. Even the massive dry dock where the thousand-foot carriers were repaired and new ones assembled. The Chinese missiles fell short of the nuclear submarine assembly buildings. A mistake the Chinese were going to pay dearly for. The other Chinese mistake was that they didn't supply the farms in Virginia with the targeting information for the Naval Weapons Storage sites. The storage sites contained sufficient weapons to fight the Chinese.

The air wing targeted the incoming drones and rockets with their AIM-9X Sidewinder heat-seeking missiles and their 20mm cannon. Two of the F/A-18E fighters decided to bump drones into the ocean. The fighters were successful in downing all but four of the drones. The *Stennis* was able to use a prototype microwave weapon that had just been installed to confuse the remaining two drones.

The air-wing circled the *Stennis*, hoping they would be able to land on their ship. The two refueling drones refueled the planes until the ship's flight deck was repaired. The captain told them he wasn't sure the ship was ready yet so they were to leave one E-2D performing recon with two fighters, and the rest were ordered to return to their base, refuel, and rearm. They were to keep four fighters on alert 5 in case the *Stennis* needed assistance.

The acting captain ordered the damage control department to draft anyone they needed to repair the flight deck and the hangar deck. The commander who was standing in for their missing captain wanted the repairs completed in five days. He ordered one of the pilots who made it to the ship to be the acting CAG (Commander Air Group) to figure out how to get his planes back on the boat. He ordered *Stennis'* Department heads to check in at the officers' mess. He realized he'd lost four of his key officers in the attack, and four others had arms, hands, and heads bandaged.

He told them. "Thank you for dropping what could be dropped on this shitty day. I don't know where the Admiral, Captain, and CAG are, nor do I know where the Chinese are. I don't know if they are waiting for us to exit the harbor, so even if they are, we're bigger than them. I want full speed. Run the reactors to 120%. If they are waiting for us, we'll ram them. One hundred thousand tons beats whatever they have. If we ram them, it won't be us getting hurt. CAG, get your birds refueled from the base and load them for bear. It's time to have one from Column A and all of them from Column B. They hurt us, we're going to show them the gates of Hell. They are weapons-free. I repeat that for the cheap seats, you're weapons free. Now let's get into the damn war."

The *Stennis* accelerated to 40 knots exiting the harbor. The captain smiled, "Lookie here. There's a damn Chinese spy ship just sitting there. OOD, ram that POS!"

"Sir?"

"You heard me. Our offensive weapons are our planes that can't operate from us because someone put a damn hole in our flight deck. I want revenge. Someone get the CAG up here."

"CAG reporting as ordered."

"CAG do you see that POS 1,000 yards in front of us?"

"Yes, sir. You want me to kill it don't you?"

"Yes, where is our wing?"

"On the way. I have four F/A-18Fs in bound at 600 knots."

"Mach is approved."

"Aye, sir."

Lt. Ryan Moore received the order. He called the other three in his wing. "On my mark go to afterburners and assume attack formation. Eagle Eye will be on my wing, Dancing Bear will lead the second flight with Ballerina on his wing. Mark!"

The four F/A-18s broke the sound barrier and flew over the *Stennis*, their home, each plane waving its wings as they flew over the damaged and still smoking carrier. Moore led the first attack on the Chinese spy ship. He dropped his two 500-pound bombs on the ship. One just missed and exploded at the ship's water line. The blast broke welds open on the port side of the ship. His second bomb landed on the ship's helicopter hangar. The explosion ruptured a fuel line, resulting in a fireball. Eagle Eye's first bomb penetrated the bridge, killing the captain. The second penetrated the bow, which blew out the side of the ship. The other two fighters' bombs struck the now-burning ship. The four planes lined up and opened fire with their 20mm cannons. The dense shells tore through the thin sides of the boat, killing half of the crew. A Coast Guard National Cutter arrived to take the surviving crew into custody.

Destroyers who exited the harbor surrounded the *Stennis* to protect the carrier, whose crew threw the book out and worked around the clock repairing the flight deck. They managed to repair the deck in three days. The hangar deck took another three. The hangar deck was useable but the doors that separated the deck into three parts had been damaged so only one door functioned.

*****

The Chinese attack on America's military bases was based on surprise. While Japan, on December 7th, 1941, didn't want a surprise attack, the Chinese MSS knew they needed one if they were to succeed. The MSS thought that by destroying the White House, the Capitol, the Pentagon, and the other bases just as the President took the oath of office, they would have achieved their goal of a successful surprise attack on America and wounded the Americans enough for them to sue for peace before things got out of hand. They hadn't counted on the ceremony being delayed because the current President was sending alert messages in the proper code to warn the bases of the now expected surprise attack from the Chinese-owned farms and warehouses. The MSS couldn't risk sending a message to their agents because the risk of the NSA intercepting such a message was too high. They had used trusted agents to hand-carry their orders.

The swearing-in ceremony had been delayed because at the last minute, the president realized it wasn't safe to be so close to the construction happening at the Capitol building, and the current president was slightly delayed while he reviewed the intelligence and his efforts to warn the soon-to-be president.

The MSS informed Xi that they had calculated the odds of the NSA discovering their plans the closer they got to the attack, and these odds were close to one hundred unless their messages were sent in one-time codes. By the time the American NSA broke the code, their flag would fly over the ruins of the White House, so they convinced Xi to approve a plan where everyone would jump off at the exact moment. They would rely on the timing to place their weapons at the same time.

Of course, Murphy had a say in the timing. No one could have thought the current President would delay the ceremony because his intelligence agencies had put the pieces of the attacks on the *Ford*'s strike group, and the suicide pilots who crashed their planes into the Pentagon, Capitol, and the White House were the first acts of a significant attack on the United States. While the delay was only a few minutes, those minutes snowballed in a way the Chinese never expected.

He agreed that the Chinese were starting their war against America. He ordered the alerts to be sent, and he attempted to reach the soon-to-be sworn-in President so he was warned and could issue the appropriate orders without being able to reach the new President who was angrier by the minute against his predecessor The soon to be the ex-president told his staff they'd done all they could do in the time they had. He asked the Secretary of War to stay behind and coordinate military actions.

The upper atmosphere winds were stronger than projected, pushing the three planes that struck the Capitol, the White House, and the Pentagon ahead of the strike time in the plan. The original plan called for those planes to strike their targets when the President was in Marine One, flying to Air Force One. The attack on Andrews went off a few minutes late while they waited for the winds gusts to die down, but Marine One landed late, and as luck would have it, an unguided Chinese rocket destroyed Marine One with a direct strike as it was landing.

The swearing-in ceremony began as soon as the current President took his seat and finished waving to everyone. The soon-to-be President made a mental note to find a way to get even with him. He whispered to his wife. "Remind me to pay him back in kind for his grandstanding and trying to steal my thunder. Today was supposed to be about me, not him. He's yesterday's news, I'm today's and tomorrow's."

His wife whispered back. "Don't worry about him. He's due to have a heart attack soon. The only time you'll have to deal with him again will be at his funeral.

You'll have to remember not to smile and have a phony tear the media can see, so they can write about your empathy. It will guarantee your reelection."

"How do you know he's ill?"

"Honey, I never said he was ill. I said he will have a heart attack. He's aged in his second term. We can't have the media always comparing the two of you. He has to be gone. His funeral will shock his supporters and leave them without anyone to look to. If you play your cards right and hold them tight to your chest, your problem will be gone in less than a year."

"A year?"

"He has nothing left. He lived to be President, but without it, he didn't age well. Trust me, he will be gone within the year. Now put on your best smile and thank him for coming." She never mentioned she had been paid fifty million dollars to make sure a clear, odorless, and tasteless drug was ready to put into his Cokes.

"Why?"

"It's a picture that will be reprinted at his funeral. It will show you to be the bigger man."

*****

Aides with the news from America and the death of the President tried to reach Xi who had left orders he was not to be disturbed, not for any reason. When his CoS finally got up the nerve to interrupt the meeting, Xi called his guards to take his CoS outside. He didn't understand why the Americans hadn't responded.

Xi checked his watch and wondered why the President didn't answer the newly installed hotline or his cell. Xi told the MSS agent in his office. "Find their damn President. If this gets out of hand, we could find ourselves in a nuclear war. The plan was always to show them they weren't the world's superpower any longer, that title was now ours. We will make his surrender look like he was signing a peace treaty, and in the five years of the absorption plan of America, they will wake to find themselves disarmed and without freedom of the press, as if they'd had that for years. The plan won't work without him answering. I'm worried their previous president somehow got to him. By the way, wasn't he supposed to have a heart attack?"

"Sir, he didn't drink the coke we spiked. He drank from an unopened can. He forgot about the glass his aide had just filled for him."

"Sir, if he won't answer..."

"Either he answers, or you'll stand against the wall downstairs along with your family."

"Yes, sir. I'll try to find a way to reach him. What about his Vice President?"

Xi shook his head. "Don't ever mention her name to me. I told the president she would help him win, but once he did, he needed to send her somewhere without the Internet and hope she gets food poisoning or has a very sad and fatal accident. One we'd be happy to arrange so he could honestly say he had an idea, and the nation should spend a week mourning her."

Xi didn't care about the loss of life; he only cared about defeating the Americans and wounding them so much they couldn't challenge China's rise to the top. He was tired of the constant excuses from the MSS. He told his admin to get the new President on the line. He didn't know they had accidentally killed the President. China had invested over three hundred million in getting him elected. It had never dawned on him that the attacks on Andrews might strike the very man they had so much invested in.

Xi's admin knocked and entered his office. He bowed to show his respect for his boss. "Sir, do you have a moment?"

"Do you have the American President on the line?"

"Sir, the American President was killed in our attack on Joint Base Andrews. One of our rockets happened to strike his helicopter as it was landing."

"How in Hell did we just happen to kill the one man on this planet who was going to surrender? Are you sure their right-wing media isn't spinning up a false story about him dying?"

"Sir, we have picked up radio transmissions saying Marine One was destroyed when one of our rockets exploded right over it as it was landing. They are even showing cell phone videos of the explosion."

Xi shook his head and ordered fresh tea to be delivered. "Where is their VP?"

"Sir, our agents reported she is in one of their tanks."

Xi broke up laughing. "They put her in a tank? I bet she's pissed she broke a nail when they pushed her in. Okay, we know she won't stay in a tank, where will she be taken?"

"Sir, we believe she is being taken to their presidential shelter, the one they call Site R."

"We have to reach her before she manages to get taken into their underground shelter because all of the comms in and out of the shelter are recorded. Find a way I can speak with her before she's taken to the shelter. Make sure you call off the sniper. We can't afford to lose her, or at least not yet." Smiled Xi.

"Yes, sir."

The US Army had left two M1A2SEP tanks at the Marine Base on 8th Ave in Washington for maintenance and repairs to their tracks after the July 4th parade. The Army sent parts and instructions detailing how to repair the tanks. Since the Marines used to operate the M1 tanks, so their motor pool techs knew how to repair them. Tanks typically require thick rubber pads to be installed on their tracks when traveling on paved roads. The two tanks had thrown most of their pads from the right-hand tracks, so they were stopped from being in the July 4th parade that celebrated America's 250th birthday.

The Marines repaired the tanks and were waiting for the Army to send trucks to pick them up when the balloon went up and America found itself at war with China. The Secret Service decided to take the tanks ahead and place the VP in a Marine helicopter, where a judge was waiting to swear her in. There's a battle going on at Site R, so she can travel the last two miles in the tank. I don't think the armed people have anti-tank weapons.

It was an excellent plan, but the newly sworn-in President refused to stay captive in a tank. She didn't understand why she had to stay inside the 70-ton monster that was hot even in the winter, and the noise was driving her crazy as she stared at the huge 120mm cannon's breach that she was leaning against and the tank commander kept telling her not to touch the breach or when the cannon is fired, she will be seriously injured, maybe even killed. He kept offering her a helmet which she refused because it would mess up her hair when the images floated around the internet of her being president and ending the war.

She ordered, as President, the driver to stop the tank so she could get out, and she'd continue the trip in one of the black Suburbans. The tank commander ordered the driver to stop. He was happy to get rid of her since all she did was bitch about everything, starting with the seats. There wasn't enough space in the tank for her, let alone a Secret Service agent, so they rode in the black Suburban that followed the tank.

The tank commander, a sergeant, attempted many times to explain to her that the tank was an instrument of war. It wasn't a limo. He had the radio operator get the Secret Service on the horn to get some sense in her. The sergeant was told the lead Secret Service agent said to tie her in a seat until they reached site R. He laughed, "What damn seat is he talking about? I guess he's never been a tank before." She yelled at him that she needed a limo and wanted it right now.

Once the tank stopped, the sergeant opened the hatch and helped her out. She had been sitting in the gunner's seat. She stood and stretched from the hours of being forced into the small compartment inside the tank. The commander smiled as she surveyed the surroundings. "Where's the stairs?"

"Ma'am, we usually jump down."

"Are you crazy?"

"Let me see what I can do. I'll talk to the Secret Service in the cars behind us."

One of the agents smiled. "She asked for steps?"

"Yes, what will it take for you to take her off my hands. If we see any action, she'll go crazy and could be a danger to all of us."

"You're right. We'll take her off your hands. When this is over, you'll owe me a big one."

"Deal. Anything to get rid of her."

They say you never hear the round that kills you. The orders the sniper had read said he had one target, the Vice President. He didn't know the President was dead, and he should have checked to make sure his mission was still a go. Without a radio or even a cell phone, he was out of communication with his upper officers. He'd been following her and prayed for the perfect shot. He had been in the country since Biden had opened the borders. He was one of the 'runaways.' He crossed with two thousand. The border agents were tied up with them, he managed to slip away and meet with his handler who was an officer in the MSS.

He was one of China's best snipers, he had never missed his target. His rifle and special ammo were sent in pieces to the Chinese embassy, where an MSS agent delivered them to him. He waited and practiced for four years. When the President pulled herself out of the tank and stood on the turret to stretch, he smiled. It was a perfect target. He slowed his breathing. For the third time since the tank had stopped, he checked the distance and made sure his scope had a perfect zero. His rifle had a custom-made suppressor that made the firing almost as quiet as a "Hollywood shooting." She never heard the one that struck her between her eyes and blew the back of her head out. The Secret Service agent was covered in blood and the President's brain. "Who just killed the President?"

The President's body fell off the tank and into the Secret Service agent's arms. The Chinese sniper packed his rifle and disappeared into the woods.

The Army sergeant was shocked. "Did we just lose another President? Two in one day, this isn't good. Without the President and her, who the hell is going to be the President, who is hopefully going to get us out of this mess? Is it the Speaker? I'm sorry it's been a long time since I was in High School."

The agent said. "The next on the list is the Speaker of the House."

The sergeant asked, "Has the new Speaker been elected yet or is the previous one still the leader?"

The agent slowly shook his head. "He's still the Leader. After six attempts, the house was still a mess. They couldn't decide on anyone, so they decided to leave the previous Speaker in place until they could come up with someone they could agree on. There are still two dozen races too close to call, and will have to undergo a recount by hand. I'm sending an extra protection team so we don't lose another president."

One of the agents said. "Better have them find a Federal Judge so he can be sworn in. What a day from Hell. Without a Speaker, the House would be unable to handle anything. The new president was furious with the party's House leader, who couldn't agree on one person. He told them to agree on someone and complete the task by the time he was sworn in. Then he was blown up.

The sergeant smiled. "So the country elected a president from one party, and now the new president will be from the other party."

The agent nodded. "If this had just been an assassination of the President and VP, it would be one thing, but we're at war, a peer against peer. Both of our countries have nuclear weapons. Pray it never gets that far because if we start tossing nukes back and forth, it's all over."

The soldiers were silent. They knew just how bad things could get if the genies were let out of their bottles. The tank commander nodded. "All we can do is pray that both sides work out how to live with each other and do it really quickly."

Chapter 9
Who let the Rest of the Dogs of War out?

Xi had promised the country that Taiwan belonged to China, and they were going to do whatever it took to bring their wayward islanders home. China had practiced invading Taiwan, and Taiwan practiced how to slow down the invasion until the Americans could arrive—adding their might to the battle. The PLA knew their only path to success was in a massive surprise attack that took Taiwan before the American Navy could arrive.

The PLA moved thousands of missile launchers to the coast. The PLAN placed their ships in positions to block the entrances to the straits that separated the mainland from Taiwan. The PLAN positioned their submarines along the paths in the Pacific most often used by the American Navy when it intended to come to Taiwan's aid. The PLAN knew they were most likely going to lose most of their boats, but the odds of at least one sneaking past the American carrier's escorts was very high. All they needed was one torpedo to be launched at the American carrier to slow them down or cause them to change course.

One small problem with their plan was that Taiwan had been watching their every move. They had access to American intelligence and images from their satellites. They knew this time the buildup of planes and ships along the water meant China was serious this time. This wouldn't be some overflights or live missile launches to scare the Taiwanese. This was going to be their invasion.

The PLAN had practiced attacking American carriers and reviewed the wargames conducted by the Americans, including a scenario where a diesel submarine managed to sneak up on a carrier. If this had been a real attack, the submarine would have been able to strike the carrier with at least six torpedoes. The submarine would have fired from a distance of less than one thousand meters, point-blank range. By the time the Americans figured out they were under attack, their mighty carrier would be sinking. The PLAN practiced their submarines to be able to sneak past the carrier's escorts and attack the carrier.

After being informed by his intelligence agency of the surprise attack against America, the President of Taiwan was worried the American Navy and Air Force had been so badly wounded they might not be in a position to assist Taiwan, so he ordered a series of actions in an attempt to make the Chinese invasion painful and very bloody for China. Xi didn't care how many died; his goal was total unification of China. The President of Taiwan smiled, thinking of turning the tides red with the PLA's blood.

The Taiwan President knew the sight of hundreds of thousands of body bags with the mangled and burned bodies of China's young men could lead to such anger that the people of China might find the means to fight for their lost sons. He ordered the Taiwan special forces to begin arming the citizens who would likely be affected by the losses. He ordered his military to take pictures of the dead Chinese troops on the beaches when they invaded and ran into the defensive fire and mines established by the military and hundreds of citizens who volunteered to help mine the beaches and the water along the most likely invasion sites.

Taiwan had plans to bring the war to China's doorstep by turning the small islands between them and the mainland into missile bases that could reach into China and also strike their invasion fleets. They had plans to turn the islands into walled fortresses to defend against China before they reached Taiwan. Unknown to China or even America, Taiwan had secretly developed its own surface-to-surface missiles. They had also developed a long-range (over 150 miles) missile that could be launched from trucks as small and light as a Toyota pickup, sort of an improvised technical. Once launched from the islands, the new missiles could strike the PLAAF bases along the border. Taiwan also fielded their updated zhdiung Feng anti-ship missiles that had a range exceeding 140 miles.

Taiwan produced thousands of naval mines. In the middle of a cold January, 18th night, six wooden hull mine layers, disguised as fishing boats, laid overlapping mine fields in the Taiwan Strait. Any invasion force would have to travel through the minefield. America donated four hundred Mark 37 mines that were taking up space in warehouses. The Mark 37 held a torpedo that listened for specific sounds that matched those in its memory. Once the sound matched, the warhead was released, the warhead was a torpedo. It would strike the targeted boat under its keel. The explosion would then create a bubble of gas that would cause the ship to rise and then fall hard back into the water, with a broken back, usually leading to the ship breaking into two sections.

America had published a note in the Department of Defense budget, it spent five million dollars to inspect and dispose of the Mark 37 miles. They didn't lie; they did dispose of the mines, all the way to Taiwan.

In addition to the mines, Taiwan placed hundreds of their home-developed (by reverse engineering the American THAAD system) SAMs. Something the Americans didn't know until Taiwan surprised a dozen Chinese planes flying over the islands on their way to Taiwan. Of the twelve planes that ran into a wall of SAMs, only two managed to return to their home base. Both were damaged by shrapnel from the exploding warheads that had missed directly striking the planes when their pilots radically turned as the SAMs approached the planes. The other ten weren't so lucky. These weren't any ordinary fighters; they were the PLAAF's stealth J-20 first-line fighters.

Taiwan had four submarines when the war began, or that was what both China and America thought. In reality, they had quietly completed two AIP prototype submarines that Japan had been contracted to supply. The decision was made to send the two into battle. Since these boats didn't have to raise a snorkel above the surface, something modern radars easily spotted, to recharge their batteries, they could remain submerged for a longer time. Only Japan knew of the existence of the boats; they would come as a rude surprise to the PLAN.

Japan knew that if Taiwan fell, Japan might be next. They offered Taiwan any assistance they could supply. The six boats silently sat on the bottom waiting for the Chinese invasion fleet they knew was coming. Each boat was loaded with additional torpedoes and food. The diesel/electric boats used a long, thin snorkel that had been covered in RAM (Radar Absorption Material) similar to the coatings on America's B-2/21 bombers. These enabled the submarines to spend more time hiding on the bottom of the straits. The RAM enabled the almost silent boats to be a surprise to the PLAN.

When the new American President began taking his oath of office, China launched its invasion of Taiwan. Fifteen troop ships escorted by twenty frigates and a dozen destroyers left their anchorage with the small islands as their initial targets. The PLA planned to use the islands as its FOB (forward operating base). The invasion fleet ran into the first minefield within a mile of leaving their bases. The PLAN had assured the PLA leadership that no such mines existed, and if they had, they would know about them, and they would send their mine sweepers out to clear the path for the fleet.

As the invasion ships ran into the mines, they received another surprise. Taiwan had purchased a large number of Exocets and Harpoon anti-ship missiles. While both were previous generations than the ones the PLAN and American Navy used, they were fired at almost point-blank range. The ships were trying to get out of the mines when the anti-ship missiles arrived. The Exocets struck the ships at the waterline, opening large holes in the hulls. The Harpoons rose, pitched over, and attacked in a vertical strike; one, the anti-missile defense guns couldn't defend against.

The ship's defenses were based on missiles at wave-top height. They knew about the Harpoons' pitch-up mode but thought their defenses could shoot the missiles down before they pitched over. They were wrong because Taiwan had programmed their Harpoons to pitch up earlier in their attack than the Americans' original programming.

Of the fifteen troop ships that started the trip, only two remained, both damaged, both were listing from the holes in their hulls, and the number of flooded compartments. They were loaded with bodies and thousands of wounded, burned soldiers and sailors pulled from the oil slick, burning water. All of the frigates were burning or had sunk from running into the mines. Only two destroyers managed to return; both had damage from the Harpoons. One's bow had been blown off when a Harpoon missile exploded in the ship's vertical missile cells. Cells that were loaded with missiles. The fires caused the Chinese missiles to explode.

The explosion tore the bow off the ship. The second surviving destroyer had been stuck in its helicopter hangar. Due to the stored weapons and fuel for the deployed helicopter, the hangar exploded. Fire found its way into the guts of the ship. Over fifty percent of the crew were either dead or severely burned.

The Generals of the PLA were furious; they ordered a massive bombing flight, as one put it, "We are going to blot the sun with the number of planes we send against them."

The Taiwan early warning planes and large radar stations that had been built on the top of mountains to increase their range, saw the hundreds of planes begin their flight toward Taiwan. The Taiwan commanding general ordered. "Unleash all of the SAM batteries. Hit them hard and fire the secret weapons in their path. Maybe this crazy idea will work. I didn't believe in it when the 'white coats' proposed it, but the President ordered it deployed, so cross your fingers and pray to your ancestors this works."

The crazy idea originated from jet engine maintenance technicians who proposed using small hot air balloons to drop bags of small rocks and shards of glass into the path of oncoming planes. The bags were held up by small parachutes or small helium balloons that slowed their descent. The bags were small, but there were hundreds of them, and they had been painted to look like small clouds. They hung in mid air and were impossible for the PLAAF's plane's radars to 'see' them. By the time the Chinese pilots realized they had run into something, the rocks and shards of glass had already been ingested into the jet engines. The material got sucked into the compressors, the rocks and glass broke the blades, causing the engines to catch fire or flame out. In either case, the pilots were forced to eject from their dying planes. Taiwan had learned how to do more with less. Taiwan's military leaders had studied the Ukraine/Russia war. They learned they would have to adopt and try new ideas very quickly.

The PLAAF lost twenty-two fighters due to the destruction of their engines. One pilot managed to make it to his base because he'd lost only one of his engines, but he was in tears when, as he started landing, his second engine seized and spat flames. He was lucky that his plane landed safely on the runway, and without engines, he couldn't put them in reverse. His plane continued down the runway until it came upon the fence that surrounded the airport. The fighter ran into the fence, and the super-hot brakes ignited the leaking fuel from the plane, striking the fence.

The burned fuel flowed down the runway, and some managed to set fire to the fences surrounding the base's fuel farm. The tanks exploded like a small nuclear weapon. A large black mushroom cloud hung over the base. The local population thought it was a nuke; they jammed the roads, blocking the local fire department from helping put the fires out.

The PLAAF had no idea what had happened. They'd never experienced so many engine failures in a single mission. None of the pilots remembered to mention the small bags that got sucked into their engines. The PLAAF tried it a second time. This time from an air force base two hundred miles inland from the PLAAF bases along the coast.

The weapons' techs cheered the success of their little project. The President of Taiwan, LongCi, smiled when he'd heard the mines, SAMs, and their stupid little bags of shit had actually worked. He knew the Chinese would quickly figure out what had happened to their planes and would install screens over the intakes to block the bags from being sucked in. It reminded him of the war in Ukraine when they mounted screens on the top of their tanks to protect them from Russian drones.

LongCi met with his military advisor. "Congratulations to the crazy techs who came up with that anti-air weapon. Can they use it again, and are we good to go with phase 2?"

Major ToGi nodded. "Sir, we're ready. The new warheads have been installed and the techs are loading their BoS weapon."

"BoS?"

"Sir, bags of shit."

LongCi broke out laughing. "A proper name. Speaking of the warheads, how many do we have?"

"Right now, we have two hundred ready to launch. Our targets are their PLAAF bases and the PLAN bases along the coast."

The order was given, and one hundred fifty missiles were launched, these weren't the typical ballistic missiles. These flew very low, similar to anti-ship missiles. When they reached their targets, they pitched up and exploded over the PLAAF and PLAN bases along the coast. Since they flew very low and used ramjets, they were very fast, Mach 4. By the time they pitched up and were spotted by the PLAAF/PLAN, it was already too late to stop them. GPS guided the missiles to their targets. Each exploded over its target, spreading sleeping gas at 0400. Most of the people on the PLAAF and PLAN bases were asleep and would now remain so for another six hours.

Chi nodded. "Launch Phase 3. Order some more of those little bags of crap. I don't think they've figured it out yet. Keep our planes out of the area. I don't want to hear about any blue on blue losses."

"Yes, sir. The planes will be in the air in less than five minutes. They were waiting for the order."

"The order is given. I'd love to see the look on Xi's face if we manage to pull this off."

Twelve C-130s took off from Taiwan air bases. Each carried 92 paratroopers who jumped onto the PLAAF's bases that had just been put to sleep with the gas. Once on the ground, they tied up the pilots and crews before they spiked the planes so they would blow up on command. They placed mines at the fuel farms and weapons warehouses. Once the officer in charge signaled success, the C-130s landed. The paratroopers ran up the rear ramps and flew back to Taiwan. Others parachuted into the PLAN's bases. Limpet mines were attached to a total of one hundred twenty ships. They also set thermite bombs in the hangars and along the walls of the mess hall and the barracks.

They smiled, thinking of what was going to happen when everyone woke up. Before leaving, three paratroopers placed bombs on the massive fuel tanks on the bases. Without weapons and fuel, the PLAN bases were useless. When the mines and bombs exploded, the PLAN was going to discover they didn't have any ships ready to carry troops to Taiwan, and many of their troops were dead from the fires the paratroopers had set.

While the Taiwan special troops planted the bombs, the PLAN issued new orders to its two carrier strike groups. One patrolled the northern and one the southern access point of the South China Sea. They knew the Americans would send submarines and their carrier strike groups to sink the Chinese invasion groups. China had sixty-six submarines compared with America's 68.

Of America's 68 submarines, only fifty-three were attack boats; all of America's were nuclear-powered. Nearly forty percent of America's attack boats were unavailable for sea duty. 40% of the unavailable boats were waiting for repair, some waited for years for a dry dock and parts. In addition to the lack of parts, there was a shortage of skilled workers. In early 2025, the Navy had started to use 3D parts to speed up repairing boats.

That left only 32 boats to provide protection for the fourteen SSBN boats and protect the carrier strike groups. That left only a small number available to perform their wartime duties. The Navy was very short of skilled people to manufacture and repair their boats. The CNO worried that when China attacked, he wouldn't have sufficient boats to, one, attack China's fleet, and two, sink their ore and oil ships that sailed through the Indian Ocean on their way to China. Sinking China's supply ships was the war against Japan updated, only now, the route was longer, and the CNO had fewer boats.

An example of the mess the American Navy found itself in, the *USS Connecticut* ran into an underwater mountain and tore its nose apart in 2021. The CNO had hoped to have the ship repaired and returned to service in 2025, and then it was expected to be available in mid-2026. Now, it appeared it wouldn't be fully repaired and updated before mid-2029. The issue was when the parts for the nose and sonar would finally be available. Some of the parts had to be made on 3D printers because there had only been three boats built in the Seawolf class, with one that had been turned into a special operations boat. Spare parts hadn't been warehoused, so everything the boat needed had to be hand-made. Example two was the *USS Boise*, which had been waiting to enter a dry dock for three years. The CNO decided to cut his losses and scrap the *Boise*, and he prayed that the 3D printing would get his boats back to sea.

The PLAN was ecstatic with their success with the sinking of America's two newest and most powerful carriers, the *Ford* and *JFK*. The PLAN planned on overwhelming the existing strike groups' defenses with drones. The PLAN had 'gamed' the attack out. They had built a one-to-one model of an American *Ford* class carrier in the desert. They used it to plan how to overwhelm the carrier's defenses and to cripple it sufficiently so that its offensive weapons, the carrier's planes, were removed from the playing field. The PLAN and the MSS knew the American strike groups had a limited number of surface-to-air missiles; when they were gone, the boats would have to reload, a very time-consuming process.

The PLAN knew some drones would manage to strike the carriers. Some always managed to slip past the defenses, none are ever one hundred percent efficient in stopping the incoming drones and missiles. The PLAN knew the Americans didn't have warehouses full of reloads. The follow-up attack would be made by the PLAN's new stealth naval fighter, the J-35, which was a very close copy of the American F-35. The PLAN had observed the Americans working out how to reload their destroyers from replenishment ships at sea. It took over an hour to replace one vertical launch cell; at that rate, it would take over 90 hours to reload one ship, and to date, only one replenishment ship had the equipment to reload the cells on the water.

The PLAN tested its plan by sending over a thousand suicide drones to soak up the Americans' very expensive SAMs from the USS *Bush* and her escorts. Many of the drones were launched from commercial fishing ships, others from cargo ships that had their drones inside of typical cargo containers. The Americans would have to respond to the threat, so ships loaded with fifty SM-6 and SM-3 missiles would quickly run dry.

When the Americans retreated to begin their reloading, the Chinese would saturate both the destroyer and the replenishment ship with drones and missiles. They knew war was won or lost on logistics. The war for the Pacific was going to be fought on China's back door, and the Americans would be at a total disadvantage with their supply chain stretched for over two thousand miles. The Americans had a limited number of replenishment ships. The carriers were nuclear-powered and could operate for over twenty-five years before requiring refueling. Without its planes, the carriers were large empty shells. Its planes needed fuel and weapons replaced. The 6,000-plus crew members needed food. Without the Navy's replenishment ships, the carriers and destroyers would have to leave the area and travel a thousand miles or more to resupply and rearm. By that time, the war would be over, and China would control the Pacific.

The PLAN planned to choke the American Navy and force it away from the western half of the Pacific. Their plan was very simple, destroy the bases the Americans counted on for supplies and repairs. The PLAN had the assistance of the PLAAF. They struck the Philippines, Midway, and, of course, Pearl Harbor. The Chinese had hundreds of ballistic missiles with a range of 2,500 miles, more than enough to travel the 1,854 miles between the mainland and the Philippines. Over three hundred missiles struck the Philippines' naval and air force bases. The missile attack knocked the Philippines out of the war. The PLAN subs sunk any Philippine ships that managed to leave port.

The PLA modified some of their ICBMs to carry high-explosive warheads instead of nuclear ones. This enabled the Chinese to strike the Midway Atolls and Pearl Harbor without risking any of their troops or planes. The Ambassador from China to America informed the commanding general of NORAD that the missiles didn't have nuclear warheads. He asked NORAD not to overreact. He urged the Americans not to rely on just their missile launch detection satellites that had already alerted NORAD to the launch. The commanding general of NORAD decided not to use his limited number of missile interceptors on non-nuclear missiles. He told the Chinese Ambassador, "If one of those missiles is loaded with a single nuke, I will unleash our entire arsenal on China."

The general believed the Chinese because he knew they knew if one of their missiles exploded with a nuclear explosion, he would order the launch of America's Trident missiles. The tension was in NORAD headquarters, located inside Cheyenne Mountain. The buildings in the mountain were built on monster springs to absorb a direct nuke. The fifteen buildings sat on 1,000 springs designed to absorb a 30-megaton nuclear explosion.

NORAD tracked the Chinese missiles and issued warnings to their targets as soon as NORAD's computers projected the missiles' points of impact. When the target circles were displayed on the main monitor the commanding general, Major General of the USAF, Kevin Blasé said. "The assholes are targeting the Navy's replenishment and repair bases. Can those bases defend themselves?"

The General, who was in command of the Pacific's defense, answered. "Sir, Midway and Pearl have a very limited number of THAADs. They were sent with the Marines to establish a missile safe zone. There is also one Burke, block 2A, equipped with the experimental laser located at Pearl."

Blasé shook his head. "Then in so many words, the Navy and we are screwed in the Pacific."

"Yes, sir. That is correct."

"What about San Diego?"

"We have issued an alert for all of the Pacific bases. I'm sure the destroyers in San Diego are on high alert, they should be able to intercept most, if not all, of the missiles. If the attack isn't from missiles, but a truck bomb, the Marines should be able to stop them."

"And if they can't stop them?"

"Sir, if we lose San Diego and Norfolk, we don't have a Navy."

Blasé shook his head. "Without a Navy, we lose the war, the Pacific, and maybe even the country."

Chapter 10

The War in the Pacific Boils Over.

The PRC's plan to remove Pearl Harbor was more than just destroying Pearl Harbor; it was devious. They had decided to break the bond of the Hawaiian Islands to the United States so they could step in and use the islands as one of their bases in the Pacific. Xi knew that once America didn't have any bases in the Pacific, it would lose all influence in the Pacific. When the American military was defeated by drones, the world would see that they had been afraid of a paper tiger. The commanding Admiral of the PLAN knew the Americans always planned to fight the last war and were now going to get caught in that mistake.

The PLAN missiles were launched from freighters slowly crossing the Pacific. The initial missiles had canisters that spread small bomblets across the bases. As soon as the initial missiles were launched, the empty containers were pushed into the Ocean. Then the tops of the next series of containers opened, and their missiles were launched. These Chinese missiles were the new hypersonic missiles that reached a speed of Mach 8.

The PRC's secondary targets in Hawaii were the dormant volcanoes. Chinese missiles struck the Navy's base at Pearl Harbor and totally destroyed it. They had accomplished in a few hours what Japan had failed to accomplish in 1941. The second wave of Chinese missiles rose and drove on to the volcanoes. Four of them erupted. The burning lava destroyed everything in its wake, and the thousands of lava bombs that were shot out of the volcanoes created more damage than the Chinese missile attack on the islands. The PRC counted on the mass destruction and the confusion of losing most of the Americans' ships, so they would offer medical assistance, food, and relocation services to the survivors. The debris from the volcanoes grounded all of the helicopters and planes.

An hour after the attack on the base and volcanoes, the Big Island was burning out of control and covered in toxic smoke from the burning fuel farms at Pearl and the airports, and of course, the erupting volcanoes. People with health conditions were falling over from their lungs being full of the volcanic ash, which was like breathing in small glass particles that sealed the airways. The panic spread quicker than the flowing lava. People stole boats in their attempt to save themselves. Some tried to drive away from the lava.

America was without a President and Vice President. None of the new administration's senior positions had been approved. The country was leaderless and totally confused. Some of the television stations carried the story of a major naval attack in the Pacific between the PRC and America. Other stations sounded the alarm that World War III had just started, which started a mass panic across the country. The governors of the Red States held a joint Zoom press conference where they told their citizens not to panic, and the Chinese were our friends.

The governor of Texas held his own press conference, where he declared a state of emergency and ordered the borders of Texas to be sealed. Other red state governors copied the Texas message; the governor of Tennessee went so far as to call up the National Guard and suggested people practice their shootings. He asked all of the shooting ranges to open earlier and stay open later.

The American Navy and Air Force bases were reduced to the commercial airports in South Korea. The USAF was working around the clock to repair the runways and look for fuel for its handful of undamaged planes. Many planes had been sent to the commercial airports, but the North had hit all of them. Crews were still repairing the runways and taxiways. Japan was warned by China. "We don't consider ourselves at war with the peace-loving people of Japan. However, if Japan decides to aid America in its fight with your Asian neighbor, then we will destroy every airstrip in your country, we will destroy every one of your cities, and we won't leave a single Buddhist Temple standing. The choice is yours, either remain neutral and live, or side with the Americans and die. We will be watching."

Japan's military thought of a third option; they sent their replenishment ships, which flew the American flag, seeking to fool the Chinese spy satellites. These ships didn't have the new way to reload the VLS system that America's escorts used. Even the new American frigate used vertical cells, which the Navy had one that had been put in action only a month before the attack. The second frigate had just been launched and, in normal times, would have taken another 18 months to join the fleet.

It was now being worked on around the clock because, with the losses, the Navy needed every ship it could get its hands on. Some naval officers suggested bringing back the reserve ships, and one went so far as to suggest seeing if the USS *New Jersey* BB-62 and the USS *Missouri* BB-63 back into service. The CNO smiled, thinking of the sixteen-inch guns tearing apart the Chinese carriers. He nodded and told an aide they should figure out if they could be made battle worthy and where the ammo for their guns was stored.

The American Navy ships badly needed supplies, reloads, repairs, and the wounded who required more aid than the ships could provide. America's Seventh Fleet had fallen for the Chinese trick; they had fired all of their SAMs at drones, leaving them defenseless against the Chinese fighter-bombers, cruise missiles, and ballistic missiles. Missiles such as the Chinese DF-2 and DF-26 'carrier killers' that could only be intercepted by the Navy's SM-3 and SM-6 missiles. The drones cost China less than thirty thousand apiece, while the missiles that destroyed them cost between 2.5 (SM-6) and 14 (SM-3 IIA) million each.

In order for the DF-21 and 26 to strike their targets, America's nuclear-powered carriers, the PLAN had to know where the carriers were. As soon as China began to strike American assets the generals and admirals who'd taken shelter in Site R ordered China's recon satellites destroyed. Using a very secret weapon, one that most had forgotten about, the easiest way to kill a satellite is to hit it with another satellite. The service chiefs agreed on reactivating the F-15 fighters that had been modified to launch anti-satellite missiles.

While the F-15s were having the anti-satellite missiles checked and mounted, codes were sent to old satellites thought to be only space junk that would eventually fall into and burn up in the atmosphere. The older American birds silently moved through their orbits according to their new orders. They plotted the right orbit to strike the Chinese eyes in space. They were either destroyed when the older satellites struck them or were bumped out of their orbits and sent drifting into space with no contact with Beijing.

With China's eyes blinded, they had to make assumptions about how America would respond. The PLA decided to launch four salvos of missiles from a different launch site. The PLA birds used their seekers in the nosecones of the missiles to scan the ocean below them. The controllers hoped they'd stumble on the American strike force. The Americans had been ordered to turn 90 degrees to the Port and increase speed, so they were out of the vision of the Chinese missiles when they reentered the atmosphere and began searching for their targets.

Some of the escort destroyers relied on an old trick, they ordered their engine crews to adjust the combustion of their turbines, so they produced dense smoke. Admiral Barrows, commander of the *Bush's* headed by the USS *Bush*, CVN 77's strike group. ordered the carrier to remain at flank speed (their highest) and every three minutes change course. Barrows silently prayed they were far enough away from the missiles' warheads when the radar tech yelled into the 1MC. "VAMPIRE. VAMPIRE. Altitude 96 angles."

Barrows responded. "Radio, Admiral, can you tell when it's acquired us?"

"Sir, I'm doing my best. They are ejecting tons of chaff, but we're assuming they've found us. I've picked up brief radio random pings. I can't figure out what they are doing, or to whom."

"Send me the files."

"Sir, they're in your computer."

"Got it. Let me study it."

Barrows told his intel specialist. "Study this report and tell me what you think, you only have a couple of seconds."

"Sir, get us out of here. The lead missile was telling the others where we are."

Barrows picked up the IMC. "Captain, get us out of here, run the reactors into the red, they found us."

"OOD, move us."

"Sir, course?"

"Second star to the right. I don't care, but make it quick and push the reactors into the red."

The Chinese missiles, twelve of them, were on their way. One had located the carrier; the others had locked onto its escorts. The carrier managed to escape from under the incoming missiles. Two destroyers managed to target the incoming missiles with their last three SM-3 missiles. Three of the incoming missiles were destroyed. Three missed the destroyers who had followed the lead of the carrier by filling the air with chaff and dense smoke while accelerating away from where the incoming missiles had targeted. Two destroyers were destroyed when they used RF generators that mimicked the carrier. They sacrificed themselves to save the carrier and crew. The destroyers used every trick they knew, an old one dating from the Cold War was inflatable rafts with RF generators and radar reflectors making the rafts look like the carrier. The rest of the missiles were tricked by the rafts and targeted them, ending the latest threat.

Barrows thanked the surviving ships and then asked the question he knew the answer to. "Does anyone have any defensive missiles left?"

The carrier's captain said. "We have six RAM block 3s. We're splitting them, three to the front port launcher and three to the rear starboard launcher. One of the weapon techs thinks we might be able to launch Sidewinders from modified RAM launchers."

"I like that idea, but if it means destroying the RAM launcher, we might have ruined our ability to reload them when we resupply. How about the rest of the destroyers?"

The two remaining destroyers answered. "Sir, we're both Winchester (Empty)."

"So, we can't defend against their missiles, and we've left the north entrance to the straits wide open. Do we have any Tomahawks left?"

The destroyers responded. "Sir, between the two of us, we have six."

Barrows smiled. "Let's play a game of poker. Launch the Tomahawks with the target area of where they pushed us out of. They must have wanted us away from there for a reason. Let's see what that reason was. Tell the birds to hunt for anything of value."

"Yes, sir."

Five minutes later, the vertical launch cell covers opened, and the long, dark gray missiles rose on a tail of fire. They pitched over and flew at 550 mph. Once they reached their waypoint, the missiles rose and scanned the area. They discovered China's newest carrier. Four missiles dove and leveled at ten feet above the surface of the Pacific. Two pitched over to strike the carrier's flight deck. The Tomahawks switched from their radar search to their thermal sensor. Something the Chinese spies hadn't yet learned. With their radars off, the target ships didn't get the warning from their threat sensors that tracked radar emissions. All six managed to strike the carrier as it was launching a strike on Taiwan. The deck was loaded with bombs and air-to-air missiles. The first two struck the carrier at the water line. They tore through the ship's hull and exploded inside the engine compartment. 1,200 pounds of high explosives tore the engine compartment apart and killed all of the crew in the area, including the ship's chief engineer and his assistant. The ship began to lose speed.

The captain ordered the planes to be launched before something else happened. That's when two of the missiles struck the flight deck. Two of the 12 fully fueled and armed J-35 fighters were struck by the missiles. The fighters exploded, sending burning debris into planes waiting for their turn to take off and attack Taiwan. In less than two minutes, all 12 were burning out of control. The fire followed an open weapons hatch and entered the front weapons storage. When the heat and pressure reached the point of no return, the missiles, rockets, and bombs exploded and tore the first one hundred fifty feet of the carrier's bow off. Two of the Tomahawks entered the hole in the side of the hull and exploded centrally in the ship. The explosions knocked the generators offline, and fires spread toward the ship's rear weapons locker.

The carrier shook from the explosions of the flight deck full of burning and exploding planes. The ship started to list from the water flowing in from the two explosions at the water level. Most of the ship's crew were tied up with fighting the fires on the deck when the explosion in the front weapons storage locker exploded, tearing off part of the ship's bow. The ship was very new, and the crew had no experience fighting a real fire that was spreading across the flight deck. The fires spread into the hangar deck where thirty planes waited their turn to take off. When the fires reached the fueled planes, they began exploding like a string of dynamite. The ship shook like a child's rattle toy when the fires reached the rear weapons locker. The heat cooked off the rocket's propellant and the hundreds of warheads. The new carrier, the PLAN's shining jewel, was finished. She's lost her bow and stern.

The captain told the Admiral. "Sir, you should transfer your flag. I believe the fires are winning and we're going to lose the ship."

"I want you to come with me."

The Chinese Admiral knew his ship was doomed. He ordered the crew to abandon the ship.

"Admiral, you know the captain always goes down with his ship."

"I, the people need you. You've got the experience we need to grow our fleet."

"Sir, I don't think losing one's first command is the experience you need. I know my choices are a firing squad or going down with my ship. I choose to go down with my ship."

"I salute your bravery. I will ask the President to name the replacement to this ship in your honor."

"Thank you. Notice the ship is sinking quickly. You've told the crew to abandon ship. That goes for you too. I have a long boat waiting for you."

"Is there anything I can do for you?"

"Find the American ship that did this to us and kill it."

"You have my word."

Chapter 11

Naval Base Norfolk is Attacked

Every ship that could, left their docks. Most simply used an ax to cut the cables that held them to the piers. America's destroyers and frigates were powered by turbine engines, very similar to those used on airplanes. Turbines spun up very quickly, allowing their ships to quickly gain speed and move into the Atlantic to join the carrier. Most of the destroyers managed to leave before the Chinese missiles arrived. However, some left with only a handful of their crew.

The situation was different when it came to the attack submarines at Norfolk. Six Virginia-class and four Los Angeles-class submarines attempted another tactic, similar to the Americans' carriers; they were nuclear-powered, and it took time for them to get their reactors up and running, generating enough steam to escape. As a result, they submerged where they were. There was just enough water for them to sit at the bottom with only their periscope, radar, and radio antennas up. The boats' engineer officer worked on starting the reactor so they would have power and could move if the captain ordered them to. Until the reactor was critical and making steam, the boats would rely on their backup batteries. The captains ordered the video captured by the periscopes to be displayed on all the monitors so the crew could see the start of World War III. The captains wanted their crews to know what they were fighting for.

Four missiles struck the base's fuel depot. The resulting explosion broke windows five miles away. A huge mushroom cloud rose into the clouds. People panicked, thinking the mushroom cloud meant a nuclear bomb had struck the base. The roads surrounding the base were jammed with traffic attempting to get away.

The *Lincoln* had recently returned and hadn't shut their reactor down yet. The captain was still on the ship when the DEFCON alert sounded. He ordered the cables cut and the ship taken out to sea. He ordered the CAG to round up his people and birds and get them back on the ship, they had a war to fight.

As the *Lincoln* began moving out of the world's largest Navy base, Chinese missiles caught her basically defenseless. The missiles slammed into the flight deck. Two broke through and exploded in the empty hangar deck. The good news was the ship was full of contractors and sailors who had been on board checking the ship for what repairs and upgrades were going to be handled in the time they had. They didn't realize they were out of time.

Lincoln's crew were able to get the CIWS and RAM missiles up. They intercepted four of the incoming missiles. The missiles had exploded close to the large ship. Shrapnel from the exploding missiles cut into the ship's hull and flight deck. Luckily, there weren't any crew close to where the missiles had exploded.

The captain asked every able-bodied crew to work with the crew from HII to cut apart the damaged areas of the deck while other teams worked to weld new sections of steel to the deck. The damaged sections were tossed overboard. Two small Coast Guard ships saw a Chinese freighter dropping mines into the channel that led the ships from the harbor to the Atlantic Ocean. The Coast Guard managed to stop the freighter from dropping any additional mines when their machine guns tore the bridge apart. Four Navy dark gray helicopters dropped twenty SEALs onto the Chinese ship.

The SEALs quickly secured the ship and discovered that ten of the twenty-foot-long containers were really missile launch containers. Each had a missile launcher loaded with missiles, like the ones that had struck the *Lincoln*. The Chinese crew were held in the mess while the officers were held in the captain's cabin. The SEALs grabbed every laptop, notebook, and the pile of notes they discovered in the captain's and the political officer's cabins. One of the teams was a safe cracker who managed to open the captain's safe. The contents of the safe were secured in bright orange bags, which were placed in rope baskets lowered from the helicopters.

The commanding officer of the *Lincoln* said a silent prayer for the Admiral who didn't make it back to the ship when it cut its cables and made for the assumed safety of the Atlantic. Helicopters buzzed back and forth from the base and the various ships. They brought crew and supplies. Some were from the *Stennis*, which was in the

HII dry dock undergoing a three to five-year SLEP. He was very glad to see his engineer officer and his XO arrive. Both were in jeans and turtleneck shirts covered by ski jackets.

The captain was told by the HII construction manager that he thought the ship would have at least two catapults running in three hours. He told the captain the arrester cables were fine. The captain said another silent prayer and thanked the HII manager. "Whatever you need, it's yours."

"What I need is some steam pipe that I don't think you have." The HII manager smiled. "While I don't walk around with steam pipes, I know where there were a lot of them. In HII's warehouse, some were tagged for the *Stennis*, my people are looking for a heavy lift helicopter to bring them here along with a special welding team and additional steel plates to repair the holes in the flight deck."

"You are a gift from God."

"I wouldn't go that far. You're smiling, does that mean you know where a heavy lift bird is?"

"I don't. But I happen to know someone who does."

He picked up the 1MC. "CAG report to the bridge. CAG report to the bridge."

A dirty Naval captain entered the bridge. "Sir, you called?"

"CAG, this fine man is from HII. He knows where replacement steam pipes and steel plates are, but he needs a heavy lift bird. Can do?"

CAG smiled. "It so happens I know where there are two we can get our hands on. All he has to do is tell me where to send them."

CAG and the HII manager chatted in the back of the bridge crew, and officers reported in. The captain picked up the 1MC again. "This is the captain. The dress for today is whatever you're wearing. Uniforms are optional. Don't waste time changing. We've got to save this old man so we can kick the shit out of some Chinese."

He heard cheers from the crew as six F/A 18E fighters flew over the deck. They waved their wings and called the CAG, "We'll be back, we're looking for targets. CAG, as soon as the deck is repaired, we're ready to come home."

The CAG smiled. "I assume you have some friends coming with you?"

"There are twelve groups of six following us. There are also three E2Ds and some refueling drones. We loaded up with weapons before we left. We'll search the area around you. Sir, what's the ROE?"

"You are weapons free for anything that looks like it's getting ready to launch missiles at us or our country. If you see a Chinese or Russian tail flag, shoot their ass down or sink them."

"Sir, that's the best ROE I've ever heard. We're on it."

Eight minutes later, the bridge saw bright flashes on the horizon. CAG smiled, "I think my boys and girls found someone of interest."

The captain smiled. "CAG, I do believe you're right. I love it when they clear the field in front of us. See if your people can stop any other Chinese vehicles within two hundred miles of us and if they find any, sink them."

CAG asked. "Any word from Norfolk?"

"They missed the air strip, but they did hit HII."

"The *Stennis* was there undergoing its SLEP."

"They got her refloated just as round two arrived. Had they not broken open the flood pipes so she could be floated out, we would have lost her. They had very poor targeting, they hit the administrative offices of HII, not the warehouses or dry docks."

"Is she able to fight?"

"Sir, I'm sorry, but I really don't know."

"It's okay. I'll reach out to whoever is commanding her once she's out here with us."

"Any word on the subs?"

"They submerged where they were."

The captain smiled. "All of them?"

"All of them. Most had cold reactors. They should be up now and coming out to keep us safe."

"That's the second bit of news I've had all day."

"What was the first?"

"You survived and made it back to the ship."

CAG smiled. "The first good news I've had is you left with a boatload of contractors from HII. They're going to repair our boat and we're going to kick some Chinese ass."

The 1MC announced. "Incoming heavy bird with a load swung under her. Looks like it's our steam pipes."

The HII engineer who'd been in the bridge with the captain and CAG smiled. "CAG, thank you. We'll have cat three up and running in three hours. Add another two for cat four. The next bird should have our steel for the bow."

CAG grabbed the 1MC, "Can we land planes while you're repairing the cats?"

"You can, if and it's a really big IF, if you can land them on the straight section of the flight deck. We'll be working on the cats on the angled deck. If you can land one and quickly take it to the hangar deck, so the deck is clear for the next one to land."

CAG looked at the captain, who nodded his head. "You're the CAG if you can time it correctly, it's good with me. There is a minor issue. The automatic landing system is down, we don't have a landing officer, and all of your pilots are up there. Do you remember how to use the paddles?"

"Of course I do. I'll get them and get busy."

"Good because it's been way too many years since I used them."

The first Hornet landed fifteen minutes later. As soon as it came to a stop, it was hooked to a tractor that pulled to an elevator to the hangar deck that was still being repaired while others were working on replacing the steam pipes that operated the catapult. Each of the four had its own steam pipe that shot the plane off the deck in a few seconds.

It was a slow process to land one plane, move it to the hangar deck, clear the deck, and repeat until all eighty planes were on the carrier. Some of the planes needed to be refueled before their turn to land. One of the E-2Ds and two of the Hornets were refueled and sent to scan the area around the carrier. Ten of their escort destroyers showed up along with six attack submarines that checked in and then began to clear the area around the *Lincoln*. The captain asked every captain if they had any information on the Admiral. None did. Two said they didn't think he made it because the executive offices of HII were hit by three Chinese missiles.

The captain of the *Lincoln* asked his CAG, "Isn't our typical load out 70 planes? If my count is right, we're currently at 80?"

"Sir, as soon as the battle damage is repaired, ten additional planes are going to land."

The captain smiled. "Are you stopping at 90 or was it a test for me. Before Bush 1, our normal loadout was 90."

"Shit, I must have lost count."

"I'm sure you know your pilots are going to have a choice, sleeping on a mattress placed on the deck or hot bunking."

"Sir, they know and don't care. They want a piece of China."

"Good. Then we're on the same side of the line. You're excused. CAG, one more question. Are you familiar with the weapons depot outside of Williamsburg?"

"Sir, of course. I assume you'd like us to send the two heavy lift birds to borrow some ordnance."

"We ended up with two SEAL teams, send them with all of our helicopters to provide support for the heavy lift birds."

The CAG looked at his captain. "Sir, expecting trouble?"

"Today, I am not taking any risks. If the Chinese are on the base, the SEALs will put an end to them."

"Yes, sir. Sir, where are they?"

The captain laughed. "They're on the hangar deck. They're helping repair it."

"This I have to see, SEALs with tools, not guns."

The captain smiled. "Don't piss them off, remember they are SEALs. I can't afford to lose you."

Fifteen minutes, twenty-four very dirty SEALs, armed with their rifles and sidearms, climbed on a helicopter and led the other birds to the weapons depot.

The captain shook his head while he tried to hide the smile on his face. *Those SEALs look like they want to find some Chinese at the depot. Oh, to be young again. I like the CAG, he takes risks, he knows what's at stake, and he tries to find a way to stop the BS. Yeah, I like him and hope he survives long enough for me to recommend he gets sent to XO school. It was a gift from God the SEALs jumped to the nearest ship they saw. Once we're loaded, I'm going hunting for Chinese.*

The SEALs saw four SUVs racing to the depot. The team leader pointed to them. "Looks like we're both going to the same place." A moment later, two bullets whizzed past his arm. "That there asshole just tried to kill me. I think we should return the favor. One SEAL sat in the open door of the helicopters. They peppered the SUVs with 5.56 mm rounds. The SUVs crashed into each other after the first one stopped so its passenger could get a better shot at the SEALs. Moments later, the helicopters circled the SUVs while the SEALs dropped hand grenades on them. The SUVs must have been loaded with explosives because all exploded. The SEALs smiled. Their leader called the Lincoln. "Captain, thought you'd like to know, we just toasted four SUVs entering the depot. They took a couple of shots at us so being the friendly SEALs we are, we killed all of them."

"Good job. Make sure the depot is secure. The heavy lifts will most likely be making a few trips back and forth."

"We'll hold the fort."

"See you soon."

Chapter 12

Texas

"Not Today Satan."

In Texas, the commanding officer of Fort Hood, General Ike Lance, didn't like the look of the Chinese-owned farm located only a few miles from the country's largest armored base. Fort Hood, just north of Austin on Interstate 35, was home to the majority of the country's main battle tanks. The Abrams Main Battle tank, M1A2SEP and M1A3SEP (the A3 versions had replaced their heavy machine gun on top of the turret with a 7.72 caliber minigun, a new generation of CAGE armor, and new smaller but more powerful reactive armor blocks mounted all over the tank in case a drone managed to get through the tank's defenses).

The SEP program had finally installed the Israeli-developed anti-missile defensive system named Trophy. Once America's defense companies got their hands on a working sample of the Trophy system, they couldn't stop improving it by increasing the radar coverage with smaller, lighter-weight radars and increased the number of unique pellets that were denser than the Israeli-developed system.

Of course, it had been almost twenty years since Israel first deployed Trophy on their tanks. Many thought the tank had no place on a modern battlefield, given the results of the losses of tanks on both sides in the Ukraine/Russia war. General Lance felt the opposite was true. He argued that infantry needed the heavily armed and armored tanks to take territory from the enemy. He said that technology can save the tank.

Lance had been operating intelligence stealth drones over the Chinese farm for a week. He told his XO something in his gut that told him something was wrong. The drones were small and almost silent. They could fly circles around the farms for eight hours. Since the Chinese radars hadn't discovered the drone, they didn't try to hide their activities at night. The American drones had thermal capability to see through rain, fog, and smoke. Thirty minutes before the swearing-in ceremony, Lance's XO told him. "Sir, the drones have picked up a shit load of action on that farm. They're moving trucks that look a lot like mobile rocket launchers. They're placing them under camo nets at the edge of their property."

Lance nodded. "Sound the silent alert. I've already increased the size and number of the rapid reaction squads. They were equipped with quick, lightly armored vehicles that would race to the Chinese-owned farm if they launched anything at Fort Hood. If the launchers rise an inch send the rapid response to pay them a visit and send Captain Plegs' group to back up the quick response team. I don't like this so let's assume it's play time."

Lane attempted to call the Pentagon, only to learn it had been leveled. He thought to himself, *BS, if they hit the Pentagon, they're going to hit us.* He waved over a staff major. "Are our people at the farms yet?"

"Sir, almost."

"Son almost only counts in horseshoes, hand grenades, and nukes. Sound the general alarm, make it no drill."

"Sir?"

"Look, we're already at Threatcon Delta, the Chinese have moved trucks to the edge of their farms, major, forget the damn book and saddle up. We're going to kick some Chinese ass."

"Sir, what if what the drone saw was something harmless?"

"Then I'll turn in my stars and your Gold Oak Leaf."

"Why me?"

"Because you're too stupid to be on my staff. Now go do some intelligence shit or whatever you do." Lance yelled, "Get the birds up and kill something. (Birds are AH-64 attack helicopters.)

As the swearing-in of the new President and Vice President was finishing up, the Chinese opened fire on the American military bases. Thousands of drones and unguided rockets were launched at the bases. As soon as the missiles were launched from the farm that bordered Fort Hood, the alarms on the base screamed. The tank crews had already been in their tanks waiting for the go code.

Lance also increased the number of land variants, the LPWS (Land Phalanx Weapon System), part of the Counter Rocket, Artillery, and Mortar (C-RAM). The Army's system was mounted on the M-113 armored personnel carrier. Lance had convinced the previous president and Secretary of War that the Army needed a better system to defeat drones and short-range missiles. The quick solution was to install the Navy's SeaRAM system, which pairs the RIM-116 Rolling Airframe Missile with sensors based on the Phalanx. Lance wanted more, so he got permission to install three batteries of the Israeli Iron Dome and Iron Beam systems at the base.

Lance ringed the base with electronic jammers to confuse the drones' computers. The anti-missile systems were placed on automatic. Jammers caused over 70 drones to either crash or fly past their intended targets. The Iron Dome, Iron Beam, and the C-RAM systems accounted for hundreds of kills. No matter how good the defense against drones and missiles looked on paper, some always managed to avoid the defensive systems and slammed into their targets. Two warehouses, which had already been cleaned out, and the mess hall were struck. The chefs were in the back washing the pots and the grill surface when the Chinese drones arrived. Only one chef was injured by the drones that crashed through the roof and ceiling, as a steel wall separated the serving and eating areas from the cooking/cleaning areas. One chef had been opening the door when shrapnel was embedded in his left arm and leg.

The rapid response teams arrived at the Chinese-owned farm as their rockets were launched from their trucks. They had responded before the alarms based on a direct order by their general. They drove across the packed-down dirt to the farm. Their very quick response took the Chinese by surprise as they were reloading their rockets, and others were starting to launch drones. The rapid response vehicles were armed with remotely controlled 50-caliber machine guns and miniguns that fired 3,000 rounds a minute. The soldiers were armed with a short-barreled version of the new M-7 assault rifle.

The Chinese were unaware of the new vehicles; they were caught off guard and paid for their lack of intelligence with their lives. In twenty minutes, Hood's quick response teams killed most of the PLA troops. They captured hundreds of drones and rockets, PLA officers, and two hundred PLA soldiers.

In Fort Worth the Chinese sent two hundred soldiers to capture the Lockheed plant that builds F-35s. The factory shared runways with the Naval Air Station, Joint Reserve Base. The Americans were alerted to the PLA's plans. The base was shared with the Marines, Air Force, Navy, and the Texas Air National Guard. The pilots ran to the line of finished F-35s that were only armed with 20 mm cannons.

The Marine version of the F-35B could take off and land vertically; they were the first to lift off and saw the Chinese convoy approaching the factory. The six fighters began strafing the convoy. One of the trucks was loaded with missiles that exploded from the 20mm rounds fired by the Marines, who were followed up by the Air Force's four F-35A planes that also were armed with only their cannons. The PLA convoy was destroyed a mile from the base. The six Navy pilots were upset they didn't get a chance to get in on the action. They began flying in increasingly larger circles, looking for anything to kill. They found one heading South on I-35, which would take them to Fort Hood.

The Navy pilots called their other partners to invite them to the party. Very quickly, the Navy pilots were joined by the Marine Corps and Air Force's planes. The sixteen F-35s completely destroyed the Chinese trucks that were loaded with missiles. I-35 was closed in both directions. The fighters turned to return to Fort Worth to refuel and see what weapons they could find, when the Navy took over the base from the Air Force that had used the base as home to two wings of B-52s, one wing of KC-135s, and a wing of F-4 fighters. The Air Force had left the Navy pilots some bombs and missiles. As soon as the F-35s landed, refueling crews and armament crews loaded sidewinder missiles and five-hundred-pound bombs on the fighters. The pilots were told the country was now at DEFCON 1 and war had been declared against China. USAF Captain link smiled and said, "Boys and girls, it's now open season on the Chinese."

The base commander told the pilots that every major base was under attack, as were some of the country's major airports. Six were sent to Huntsville, where the Chinese were trying to take over the Redstone Armory. Four were sent to the Pantex plant, located twenty miles from Amarillo, which was the country's primary nuclear weapon assembly factory. The PLA had three convoys on their way to the plant. The F-35s had the sun behind them. The Air Force pilots had the most practice dropping bombs so they were the ones sent to protect the plant. When they left, the three convoys were smoking debris on the road.

Chapter 13
Joint Base Langley-Eusti and the Naval Air Station Oceana

The closest Chinese farm the Joint Base Langley-Eustis (it was a unique installation that combined the U.S. Air Force's Langley Air Force Base and the U.S. Army's Fort Eustis.) Langley is home to Air Combat Command and plays a crucial role in maintaining air superiority, while Fort Eustis serves as a vital logistics and transportation hub. The Chinese were only interested in destroying the Air Force's Langley base and its fighters. The farm waited for the launch signal, timed to coincide with the President's swearing-in. The PLA colonel watched planes being launched and jumped the gun, he ordered the unguided rockets to be fired at the base. He wanted to be the first to claim he had accomplished his task before any of the other officers.

Three hundred fifty-five rockets struck at the same time. 50 fifth fifth-generation fighters were destroyed, and another twenty were damaged. The fuel farms were destroyed. A massive mushroom cloud rose above the base, causing mass panic among those who lived within ten miles of each base. They thought someone had attacked the base with a nuclear weapon, and the effects of the explosion would be in their neighborhoods within an hour. People filled their cars with their families, food, water, and if they had them, guns and ammo.

The surviving F-22s and F-35s followed the smoke trails back to their launch point, then they completely destroyed the trucks, reloading equipment, and the troops providing security for the launchers. Four F-35s dropped fuel-air explosive (FAE) weapons over the farm. The FAE bombs sucked the oxygen even from the PLA's lungs. When the fires burned down, nothing living was left alive on the first farm.

The farm that was close to the Naval Air Station Oceana opened fire and learned they had a problem. The targeting officer had made a critical mistake in calculating the distance from the farm to the base. Most of his missiles missed the base; the few that did strike it landed on the grass between the runways. The other missiles landed in the Atlantic Ocean.

The base had received the DEFCON 2 message and had rushed to get as many planes off the ground as possible. Many of the planes had whatever armament was in their hangars. Some had air-to-air missiles, while others had five hundred and two thousand-pound bombs. Some carried the new air-launched AIM-174 (An air-launched version of the ship-launched SM-6), and some carried two or four 70mm Hydra missile pods, each holding seven missiles.

The ones with the Hydra pods struck the launch trucks, reloading missiles and the barn they were hidden in. The Chinese farm was a crater-filled smoking ruin when the planes received orders to begin landing for refueling and rearming.

The PLA had forgotten or had simply dismissed the idea that there were armed citizens who would enter the battle. Very soon after the first missile was launched from the Chinese farm, pickups, ATVs, motorcycles, and just average cars drove through the gates of the farm, and armed citizens, many of them veterans from the GWOT, formed V-shaped groups that slowly advanced into the farm. Some had armored vests, and some had helmets. All carried what the media called 'assault rifles.' They carried AR-15s in either 5.56, 300 Blackout, and some had new rifles chambered in 6ARC. All had at least one pistol strapped to their thighs. All wore glasses and earplugs. They were led by Marine Lt Colonel (retired, but once a Marines, always a Marine) John Yamata. His grandfather fought in Europe in the Second World War, his father fought in Panama, and he had served three tours in Iraq and Afghanistan. Most of the first wave of citizens were members of his gun club.

Yamata owned a large farm on the opposite side of the Naval Air Station. When he saw the first missile's smoke trail, he told Siri to alert everyone on his local contact list. His message reached his club members, who forwarded the message to five other groups. Yamata's message was also received at their local shooting range. The manager used the loudspeaker. "Cease fire. I say again cease fire. What I'm about to tell you is the gospel truth. We're being invaded. Many of you know LT Colonel Yamata. He just advised us of the situation. He's asking for anyone with a weapon and experience to join him in kicking the shit out of the Chinese.

"The range is willing to donate ammo and magazines to whoever wants to go. Just load up on whatever you need. If you're coming, pack up. I'm going to close the range as soon as I can get my gear. I'd say you have three minutes to decide. If you want to join us, be in the parking lot, and we'll convoy to the meet up with the Colonel."

Twelve people, plus the staff of five who worked at the range, loaded their range bags with magazines and ammo. The manager hooked up straps in the back of his pickup so he wouldn't be thrown out when the truck hit potholes. He had mounted his Class III machine gun on a mount in the pickup's bed. He'd turned his Toyoda pickup into what was called a 'Technical' by the military. He picked up a loudspeaker. "Listen up. This isn't going to be 'Call to Battle.' This is the real shit. When you're hit today, you could die. There's no do-overs or oh-shits. These targets will be shooting real bullets at you. They'll be moving as you will. Follow the Colonel's orders. He's been in deeper shit than all of us combined. If you're still game, follow my truck. If not, no hard feelings."

All twelve decided to follow the Colonel. They were joined by over two hundred angry people who didn't like the idea of their homes being invaded, either. When the Chinese Colonel heard armed men and women were assembling at the gate, he laughed. "They think this is like one of their video games we sold them. Let them come, at the first sign of one of them falling, they'll go home. We have nothing to fear from them. They're playing war while we're experts at war."

The PLA troops smiled and nodded. Had they known citizens were being led by one of America's most decorated veterans, they might have felt differently. Yamata led his people silently. Many of his people had suppressors on their rifles. The number of suppressors in private hands had increased over twentyfold when they were removed from the ATF's Class III weapons list and no longer required paying a $200 fee and asking the ATFs permission to take the suppressor across state lines.

Over fifty of the people were armed with short-barreled weapons chambered in 300 Blackout and had suppressors. Twenty of them surrounded the colonel, the others used the trees, farm equipment, and their trucks as cover. The 300 Blk suppressed round being fired from a short barrel with a suppressor was almost 'Hollywood Silent' (just a soft pew). They moved from trees, bales of hay, tractors, anything they saw that provided some cover as they made their way to the missile-launching trucks.

Yamata had placed his best snipers in trees and on the roofs of some trucks. They were armed with bolt-action rifles that were used to compete in precision long-range shooting. Some of the snipers were a mile away. The snipers had high-powered scopes and special ammo that allowed them to reach out and touch a Chinese a mile away. Most of them fired the 7mm PRC (Precision Rifle Cartridge) that was designed to reach out a mile and ring an 8" steel target.

Reach out, they did. The sniper expert from the club had been a Marine sniper in Afghanistan. He was credited with 127 kills; his first round ended the colonel. He was dead from a headshot before his body fell over. The round entered the colonel's face and exploded out the back of his head along with most of his brain. Yamata led a group of twenty with another hundred who were going to hit the Chinese from their flanks. Yamata had placed his people in a V shape to hit the Chinese in a kill zone. The Chinese were shocked when they saw their colonel fall from a headshot. They hadn't heard the round that killed their leader because he had used a suppressor and was a half a mile away. The sniper began working his way down the Chinese officers and then their NCOs.

The PLA troops began to panic as they watched their officers fall without hearing any shots. The PLA troops guarding the trucks lost their courage, and many began to run for cover when Yamata led his core twenty with another fifty behind them, and they hit the guards. As Yamata's people were cleaning up any surviving Chinese, he heard a sound he said he'd never forget: fighter planes. "Everyone, hold up those American flags. Those are our planes. Get away from the Chinese trucks."

The PLA troops laughed when they saw the Americans retreating. They didn't realize they were retreating because a larger threat to the PLA was coming. A threat they weren't prepared to deal with. They hadn't been given air defense weapons because Beijing didn't believe any American planes would be able to take off. They must have forgotten about the Marine version of the F-35. Vertical take-offs and landings that didn't require a runway to take off or land. The Chinese attack on the air base had missed the hangars and runways.

F/A-18s and F-35s destroyed the missile trucks, then they overflew the Americans. The fighters waggled their wings in a salute to the Americans. Yamata lined up fifty of his shooters and had them bow to the fighters who turned upside down before streaking off looking for new targets.

Armed Americans were the world's largest army. They owned over four million weapons and more than a trillion rounds of ammunition. Many were combat vets. Some going back to Vietnam, and the majority fought in the GWOT. The Chinese had woken a deadly dragon who had slept for over 200 years. The dragon was armed, awake, and angry. The dragon wanted to feast on Chinese blood. Many simply showed up at National Guard Armories asking if they could help. Others drove to their nearest military base and said they were reporting for service. The commanding officers were unsure how to utilize them, but they could always use more personnel who were skilled shooters with their own firearms and ammunition. Most of the officers told their quartermasters to get some uniforms, boots, helmets, backpacks, whatever they needed.

Many members of the armed forces were watching the ceremony as the new president was sworn in. They were surprised when the initial rockets landed simultaneously with the screaming DEFCON alarm. The members of the military jumped up to get ready to answer the orders they knew were coming. At the same time, the Chinese missiles began to explode, rocking the bases and killing any unlucky enough to be caught in the open when the missiles arrived.

After the initial explosions, soldiers and airmen ran to their armories to fight whoever was attacking them. Sailors raced to the nearest ship if they couldn't find their own. Mechanics rushed to ensure the equipment under their responsibility was ready for war. Fighters took off to patrol and protect the nation's closed airspace. Any plane found to be breaking the FAA's and DHS's order to close the country's airspace was escorted by a couple of fighters who ordered them to land. Bombers were moved to their nuclear bunkers, which began the process of arming the fleet of B-52s, B-2s, and the handful of operating B-21s with nuclear-armed cruise missiles and gravity bombs

There were thousands of reports of missile exhaust tracks from the Chinese-owned farms. People around the country responded to the attacks by shooting most of the Asians they saw. Armed civilians assisted the military by providing the soldiers with their firepower, and they informed the officers about what they observed at the Chinese farms. Hundreds of armed citizens raced to the farms on their own and shot everyone they saw. Their fierce attack took the PLA on the farms by surprise.

Eight of the Navy's LCS ships managed to leave NSF before the rockets arrived. Four of them were equipped with the new anti-mine equipment. They quickly deployed their mine-hunting equipment as they tried to dodge the incoming rockets. Two of the boats were struck by two rockets each. One managed to put out the fires and continue hunting for mines. The second boat wasn't as lucky. The two missiles that struck this boat had exploded in the boat's rocket canisters on the bow. The explosion tore the bow off the ship. The second missile exploded inside the helicopter garage. The helicopter was in the process of being fueled and armed with two torpedoes. The follow-up explosion tore the small ship apart.

The surviving LCSs went mine hunting from the harbor and a half a mile into the Atlantic. The Block 3 mine detection system worked as designed; the LCS captains were surprised that the new equipment actually worked. The system worked by dragging sleds that cut the chains holding the mines just under the surface. Once cut, the mines floated to the surface, making them easy for either sharpshooters or the ship's 57mm gun to hit them, causing them to explode.

What the Navy hadn't expected was that these mines were daisy-chained; when one exploded, all of the mines in its chain also exploded, so other ships or helicopters that dragged sleds and flew very low over the surface were destroyed. Only four helicopters from the original twelve survived. But NSF was open to the ocean. The fires in the base and warehouses were quickly put out. The missiles targeted at the Naval Air Station were either intercepted or missed the hangars where the F/A-18s and F-35s were already taking off looking for targets. The pilots were furious that the Chinese dared to attack them on their home soil and had killed the President.

Lincoln's crew and contractors that happened to join the ship by helicopter, which kept picking people up and dropping them on the ship. They worked around the clock to put the ship back in the war. The captain read the report. He told his XO and CAG who had joined him in the bridge that overlooked the flight deck, "We have a crew, not all from our boat, but we have a crew. The reactor wasn't damaged, so we've got power. The repair crews worked a miracle. They managed to repair all four of our CATs. The arrestor gear works so we can launch and recover planes.

"They even managed to weld in replacement steel to the damaged bow. We don't have a spare cable for the arrestor, so let's try not to break the one we have. The middle bulkhead and blast doors in the hangar deck were damaged. They're still working on them, but in the end, we may lose the ability to have three separate areas in the hangar. Since the offices of HII were hit, if we run into any problems, we'll have to pray that Mayport can repair us. The heavy lift birds have reloaded our weapons bins. They also managed to pick up some sailors and some retired old salts who want to help, so we have a very mixed crew. XO, I want you to get your assistant to figure out the best areas to assign our new crew to.

"The other interesting thing is we're about to be joined by the *Stennis*. They got her reactors hot, but she's got no radar and limited comms. Her cats and arrestor gear haven't been tested. She has two CIWS systems and two RAM launchers, that's the good news; the bad is while she has the launchers, she doesn't have any missiles. Her captain and XO didn't make it they were both caught in the attack on the HII offices. We have the ammo and missiles thanks to the trips to the weapons depots. We need to get them to the Stennis and a count of how many are on the ship. XO, you just got yourself promoted to captain of the *Stennis*. I'm sure the LT who was their weapons officer will be pleased to see you. Once you get a count on what you have, let me know who you need. Between us, we should be able to make up working up crews for both ships. Go easy on their DC teams, they'd been working around the clock to put the ship back together. She was due for her SLEP, so miles of cables were in the process of being replaced. It's a major miracle that she can float, launch, and recover planes. Do an inventory of what works and what doesn't.

"The fools couldn't shoot straight. They hit the runways and taxiways at the NAS, but they missed the planes. Our people are experts at repairing runways, so we have planes. The *Stennis* had unloaded her ordnance and all of her normal supplies, they have no food, no coffee, nothing. We need a replenishment ship to fill them up with everything. There were two ships at the base. One was riding high and the other low. Neither had a crew that I know of. We need to get the one riding low out of the harbor and deliver their supplies to the *Stennis* and us. We should take everything they can give the two of us."

The CAG said, "I sent some of our mixed air wing back to the NAS so the repair crews had more space to work. Our arrestor should be able to trap our planes. We can arm the Hornets that we send to the *Stennis* so she has some initial weapons.

"They are getting loaded out as we speak. They're going to do a couple of sweeps around us before they land. They're going to be landing heavy, so we have to be very careful. Neither the *Stennis* nor us knows what our cables can take. Most of our planes are already here. Captain, get used to your new rank. I suggest you land a couple of Hornets, empty, to see how the arrestor works, then try one of the E-2Ds, and finally a fully loaded Hornet. We know they managed to repair the arrestor hydraulics on the *Stennis*, but they didn't test them. We tested ours with naked birds. We need to figure out a way to test the cables before a plane goes overboard with everything they're carrying. I'm hoping one of the E-2s can find us a target. I want revenge. I want to kill whoever hit us. CAG, see if you can locate the two of us a couple of spare cables."

The CAG nodded and smiled. "Sir, my crew shares your desire for revenge. The cables should be in the massive parts warehouses but to be honest, I don't know which one."

The captain smiled. "Today is your lucky day. One of the sailors who jumped onto the birds bringing us crew was a supply LT. Find him and get him back to the base with some security. I'm sure he can show us where there are spares for everything we ever thought we'd like to have on hand."

"Sir, do you know his name?"

"Nope. All I know is the scuttlebutt said we have a supply officer somewhere on the ship. I hope he's checking out our spares so he can tell us what he has and we need."

The CAG thought. *I think I just became the XO in addition to being the CAG.* "Sir, we'll find us a fat target."

The captain smiled. "CAG, the *Stennis* is without their CAG, I'll give you a choice, where do you want to serve, on the *Lincoln* or the *Stennis*?"

"Sir, I started with you, I'd like to see it through with you."

"Thank you. XO, that leaves you without a CAG, see who's your senior pilot and if you like him, promote him."

The newly promoted XO said. "I think we should say a silent prayer, our cables hold, and the replenishment ship can find a crew and get us back in the war."

One hundred hands were rounded up and asked to help man the replenishment ship so it could reach the carriers that had managed to make it to the Atlantic. The Hornets flew escort for the two E-2D AWAC planes whose electronically steered radar searched for any threats. Such threats would be checked out by the Hornets and/or the Lightning IIs.

The Air Force had scrambled their alert fighters, F-16s, to fly CAP over the nation's fifty largest cities. Four commercial airliners were intercepted approaching Manhattan's JFK International Airport. The F-16s flew along the airplanes and told the pilots over Guard to follow the F-16s to an airport on Long Island, where the passengers would be detained and pilots arrested for not following the NOTAM.

One of the planes was a Chinese National Airline plane. The F-16s that intercepted the plane noticed all of the window shades were down, and the pilots refused to answer the fighter's call on Guard. The lead F-16 pilot noticed the Chinese airline pilot was looking straight ahead. The F-16 on the copilot's side remarked to the lead that the copilot seat was empty. The lead F-16 pilot continued to try to get the pilot to respond. He reported the situation to his controller located at the Cheyenne Mountain Complex.

The F-16s got the one message they dreaded ever seeing. The message was short and to the point. "Shoot the plane down. Intel is the plane is a suicide plane, might be carrying an EMP device. Repeat, weapons free. Splash the plane. Confirm code 1000."

The lead pilot told his wingman. "I'll do the dirty work. Climb and continue responding to calls to investigate other planes."

"Sir..."

"I've got it. Return to the AWACs. We can't afford to lose her."

"Yes, sir."

The lead F-16 slowed his plane until he was on the tail of the Chinese plane. He locked two Sidewinders on the plane's hot engines. The missiles pinged the pilot, confirming they had a lock on the target. He smiled and called out as he pressed the 'Fire' button twice. "Fox One, Fox One."

The two missiles were locked onto the Chinese plane before they left the F-16's wings. They flew into the plane's two jet engines. The engines exploded, sending the plane into a nose-down dive to the ground. When the plane struck an empty field, the F-16s were rewarded with a massive explosion and a huge fireball where the plane crashed. The lead F-16 pilot told his wingman. "I think we just got our proof that the plane was a suicide flight. I don't know what its target was, but let's make sure there aren't others also trying to bomb us."

The AWACS called the two F-16s. "Contact, two heavies, angels 25, speed 550, heading 270. Investigate, and if suspicious, you are authorized to splash them. You have weapons release. Weapons are green. Copy?"

The lead F-16 replied. "WILCO. Two heavies, angels 25, speed 500. Heading 270. That direction will take them over D.C."

"Confirmed. You are authorized to use afterburners and break Mach."

"WILCO."

The two F-16s accelerated to Mach 1.5 (1,100Mph). They kept their radars on standby and used the data the AWACS sent to their planes on Link 16. The lead pilot said to his wingman. "They look just like the one I just splashed."

His wingman nodded inside his cockpit. "I'll take the one to our right, you can have the one on our left."

"Roger. Don't screw with these guys, we don't know if they're packing or just manned bombs. I'm going to use mine for practice with my gun."

"I like it. I could use some practice too."

Both fighters fired a short burst of 75 20mm rounds that destroyed one of the plane's engines. The Chinese plane tipped over and dove to the ground. The high G forces of the turn and dive tore the damaged wing off the planes. Both crashed into Chesapeake Bay with a fireball from where they crashed.

The lead pilot called the commander on the AWACS. "Any idea where they're coming from? They couldn't make it all the way from China. Second point, we're going to need some go-go juice or we're going to quickly go BINGO."

"Esso is in the air, ETA ten mikes. Where they're coming from? Hold on to your straps. There's a rumor that they took off over Greenland and are using it as a base to strike us."

"Where are our buddies in NATO? We've been attacked!"

"They're waiting for a president to officially declare Article 5 is in effect."

"I think that's the last straw. We should have pulled out and let them deal with the threats by themselves. I guess they're waiting for the Chinese to invite them to visit, how peaceful their invasion has been. Today I wish I were the pilot of a B-21. I'd jam Article 5 so far up their asses they would be spitting it out for years."

"Unofficially, I agree with you, but we've got to play the cards we've been dealt."

"Speaking of the president, who is our president?"

"According to the line of succession, the next person after the VP, and thank you China, for helping us duck that bullet, it's the Speaker of the House. They're checking the bodies at the ceremony. No one remembered the Speaker being there. The rumor is, he was ill and was checked into Walter Reed last night. A reporter who knows a doctor at Reed, married to her, was told the Speaker was poisoned. The Secret Service and Marines are guarding the hospital. Everyone else was moved to another hospital. He is supposed to be giving a speech tonight at 7 EST."

"Oh shit. If that can be proven, someone made a serious mistake. They wanted him out of their way so they could deal with the Senate Leader."

"Shit. I don't trust the leader. If I were dying of thirst, I wouldn't take water from him. He's a snake. How serious is the speaker?"

"We don't have any additional information. Every time I inquire, I'm told to fly my mission and leave the rest to the chiefs who survived and are at Site R."

"What about the previous president?"

"He's in his plane with his family and a few very close aides. They're flying large circles over the ocean, waiting for the dust to settle."

"We were updated that there are small wars being fought over each of the Minuteman silos, and the Navy managed to get eleven of the fourteen Trident boats to sea."

"At least they managed to get them to sea. That's eleven, each armed with twenty-four birds, each armed with four warheads for a total of 1,056 warheads, for ladies and gentlemen in the cheap seats a total of 501,600 kilotons. Enough to say goodnight, Alice. I don't think Chinese food is going to be very popular after this."

"Pray it doesn't turn that nasty, they can hurt us in the same way."

"I'm placing my bet on the Navy being able to locate and kill their boats."

"Don't forget Greenland. They could turn it into a massive missile base using their mobile ICBMs."

"Don't remind me. I've got to go, our Esso station is here. I wonder if they'll clean my canopy this time."

The commander in the AWACS smiled. "Don't push your luck. I bet your Visa can't handle the bill for this fill up."

"All I wanted was my canopy cleaned and my oil changed while I waited."

The commander laughed with the pilot. He understood the stress the fighter pilots were feeling. The humor was a way of trying to deal with the stress of combat, never knowing if there were passengers in those planes or if they were just empty planes loaded with fuel and explosives. "If you're done flirting with the refueling pilot, have a new mission for you."

"Send it."

"You've been ordered to fly alongside the previous president's plane and protect it from anyone trying to shoot it down."

"Okay, send the coordinates."

The two F-16s turned to meet up with the former president's plane. The president sat in his conference room reading reports from the chiefs. He looked up and into the eyes of his Secretary of War. "They took Greenland? How the hell did they manage to pull that off under our noses?"

"Sir, they dropped paratroops on the three airports and the main base the Navy used. We had withdrawn our planes and ships when their council and Prime Minister asked us to leave because they thought we were preparing to invade and take the country."

"Why would they do that?"

"They were concerned you intended to make Greenland one of their states."

"What about NATO?"

"Sir, none have answered our call for support due to our intent to take Greenland. NATO said that they needed the president to officially declare Article 5, and then they would debate it and get back to us. Privately, I was told they didn't want to get involved, and this was an issue between us and China."

"I see, and the new President?"

"Sir, he and the VP are assumed to be dead. Next in line was the Speaker. I know he wasn't at the ceremony. He was taken ill from something it was assumed he had eaten."

"Is he being protected?"

"Sir, the Secret Service and Marines have moved all of the patients to other care facilities. There are a couple of hundred armed people protecting the hospital."

"When can I speak with him?"

"Sir, he was asking the same question. He would like to speak with you."

"Please set it up."

Chapter 14

The War on the Internet.

The Internet was flooded with reports, pictures, and rumors of mushroom clouds over some of the country's military bases. People posted images of the smoke trails from the farms located close and sometimes next to the country's military bases. Rumors of an all-out war consumed the Internet.

Minutes later, social media was full of reports of fighter planes attacking the Chinese-owned farms. People who lived close to the farms reported that their windows had been broken, and it felt like a series of earthquakes. People reported they had been shopping when the store's shelves shook, knocking cans and boxes off the shelves.

Many of the radical Muslims who'd been allowed into the country decided this was the perfect time to take control. They killed six mayors and attacked over twenty Jewish synagogues. Most of the American Jews were liberal and didn't own guns. Their salvation came from armed neighbors who protected their streets. Some of the Muslims tried to rush the armed citizens. After all, they were just regular people playing war. That mistake took hundreds of people's lives. Videos flooded the internet claiming the gun crazies had killed peaceful Muslims in cold blood. Over fifty Mosques were burned to the ground. The armed citizens refused to allow the local fire departments to put the fires out. Social media sites were flooded with claims of a religious war being fought in many cities.

China understood the power of the Internet and social media better than anyone else. They had developed and 'hooked' hundreds of millions around the world in sharing, reading, and watching videos on TikTok. Once installed, the app mined the phone for all of its stored information, including the users' banking and personal information. The MSS learned all of the users' secrets. They were experts at using the information to blackmail politicians. When the attacks began, the MSS stole billions from the accounts of the users of TikTok. The MSS had gotten the banking information from the TikTok app that had sucked all of the login information from the phones.

Millions received emails from their bank informing them of low balances in their accounts. When the customers called their banks, they were shocked to hear their accounts had been emptied within seconds and their accounts had been accessed by their smartphones and opened with their logins and correct passwords. The victims had no idea how their phones could empty their accounts when they hadn't opened their banking app. The banks told them there was nothing they could do since the accounts had been accessed with their passwords. Billions of dollars, Euros, and other currencies flowed into the MSS's accounts. Most of the stolen funds were used to pay for the weapons used in the war.

The MSS had developed a method that allowed a TikTok user to make payments to or from any bank or credit card stored on their phone, but these payments were intercepted before reaching their intended destination when the issuing bank's fraud departments blocked many of the phony purchases. The MSS then went after the users' PayPal and Venmo accounts.

China learned from Hollywood how entertainment could be used to control and sway how people viewed events. In the year leading up to the war, China flooded its home market with patriotic war movies extolling the PRC in the best light. While the MSS didn't outright ban foreign entertainment, they strongly encouraged Chinese to purchase tickets to movies financed and produced by the CCP, which usually meant edited by the MSS. The MSS used animated movies with a high amount of action and bright colors. They bent China's history and retold the story of China's place in the world. A position stolen by the USA.

The MSS used the entertainment to convince the citizens of China and later all of Asia, and slowly even in America. Any producer who wanted Chinese funding quickly learned there were 'certain' rules to the Chinese investment. One such law was that China could never be shown as starting wars or mistreating any POWs they held. The MSS made movies showing how badly the Japanese treated the Chinese people in the Second World War.

The MSS examined Hollywood's patriotic movies and then adapted the stories to portray China in the best possible light. The antagonists were usually Americans or Japanese. Six months before the PRC's attacks, the MSS flooded the country with very patriotic movies. The MSS had produced movies over a period of five years. They held onto the movies until two months before the start of the war. Months before the attacks on America and its allies, China's movies broke one-day receipts records.

The night before the attacks on America's military bases, the MSS flooded the social media sites with 'deep fakes' of the president signing a new trade treaty with China and next he had an executive order pre-signed and postdated ordering the military to prepare for war with China with the goal of the war being China broken up into between three and five new countries.

The PLA and MSS had previously prepared videos and recordings from the Internet influencers asking their followers not to believe the phony stories that China struck first. Deep fakes and stock videos, many available on the American Department of War, were created showing the US Navy sinking over a hundred Chinese-owned fishing boats. Video clips showed American war planes attacking and sinking already decommissioned destroyers and a Russian aircraft carrier. The Russian ship was retouched to resemble one of the PLAN's ships.

The propaganda made the case that America had struck China first. China hadn't done anything to America. It had accepted the harsh and, in the MSS's words, overly onerous conditions designed to hurt China's industries and make millions of Chinese unemployed. The message was clear: 'America was a threat to the people of China.' Two hours before the attack, Xi held a very rare open press conference where he projected the 'deep fakes.' He wanted the 'proof' in the public domain to justify their attack. The masterpiece of the MSS 'deep fakes' was a grainy video of the soon-to-be President signing an executive order dated January 20, 2029, declaring war on China.

Most Chinese, like everyone in the developed world, sat in front of their TVs and computer screens, getting informed with what their government wanted them to know. Many wondered if any of their friends or members of their families were harmed in what most were calling the attacks, and the smoke trails had to be the start of the Third World War.

The Chinese didn't like the words, 'Third World War,' so they ordered their servers to change the words from 'Third World War' to 'America's Offensive Against Asian People" (AOAAP). Internet influencers quickly jumped on the bandwagon and spread the message that the war was started by the Americans, and the Chinese were taking great pains in targeting only military facilities, unlike the Americans.

The young and those who were easily swayed added their voices to the message. Thousands in hundreds of cities took to the streets protesting America's preemptive attack on China and other Asian countries. America didn't have a president, nor a VP, nor a Secretary of War or DHS. There wasn't anyone to give orders to the NSA to block the Chinese messaging.

Vice Admiral Randolph Torn was the Director of the NSA. He was briefed on the Chinese messaging. He knew the President had died at Andrews. He knew the VP was shot by a sniper and the Speaker of the House was in critical but stable condition in Walter Reed.

Torn looked at the faces of his executive team, who sat around the conference table in the executive wing of the NSA's headquarters building in Fort Meade, Maryland. "Without orders from the executive branch, we'll have to make the decisions for those who are not with us. Therefore, and I want everything I say here to be recorded, I am ordering the complete shutdown of TikTok and any messages from China. I want the truth on people's screens, I don't want to see our people falling for some BS messages from the people attacking us. Those assholes have turned truth upside down and are blaming us for the war. They are sending out fake images of the *Ford's* reactors melting down and sending clouds of radiation around the world.

"They are setting us up as the enemy of the world. They are claiming we started the war and they responded to protect the, in their words, 'The peace-loving people of the world.' They hacked our systems and stole more data than I can imagine. It's past time we stopped standing by and letting them kill the people and the country we love. I, for one, am too old to learn Chinese. I don't even like Chinese food."

The staff smiled and nodded their agreement. Torn looked around the table. "I want those assholes shut down, I want it to happen yesterday." Fingers flew over keyboards while Torn sipped a fresh mug of coffee. He looked over his shoulder at the number of sites being taken down and the number of messages, posts, and pictures being edited or rewritten. "I want the truth to flow from every screen. Once that is accomplished, I want their internal systems down. Let's see how they like being in the dark, and their ATMs pouring money into the street. Use the new system that was recently installed in the basement to get into their military's systems. See if we can change their targeting from us, back at themselves. Use Stuxnet Block ten to destroy their control systems in all of their factories. I want to hear Xi on the phone asking for a truce. Now get to work, we have a nation to save and one to teach a lesson to."

Torn's director of the Internet asked. "Sir, what if the truth shows us in a bad light?"

"Everyone, listen up. When I said I want the truth, I meant the truth. Not the truth you believe it to be. The only way to defeat China in social media forums, chats, images, and interviews is to let the truth rise to the top, and in some cases, help it do so. Remember, in fresh milk, the cream always rises to the top. I want us to get the truth out there. If you're not sure of what is true, then check it, and if in doubt, ask me. My door will always be open to discuss the truth. Now, if there aren't any further questions, let's get back to work. The MSS has had a huge head start, pouring 'deep fakes' into every social media site. Let's teach them a lesson. You have authorization to spike any site or post that originated from or was hosted by one of the MSS's servers." The room emptied, leaving Torn alone with his thoughts and misgivings. *The definition of truth depends on which side of the dateline you're standing on. Only the winners get to write the history of the war. In this case, it has to be us.*

Facebook and Instagram were both owned by the same company, which, like many tech companies based in Northern California, strongly supported China's version of the story. The Admiral was torn, funny, he thought, because that was his name, between free speech and the truth. He decided the truth had to overcome China's claim of free speech. He sent a quick note to the team watching over the two companies. "Make sure you keep both of your eyes on FB and Instagram. The MSS's message is deeply embedded in their editorial comments and censoring. If the only way to get the truth out is to turn FB and Instagram off, then do it. I'll sign the order so the axe only falls on me."

Slowly, the truth began to spread through social media sites. The major influencers noticed the small change. They started to switch sides when Torn approved paying them for posting the truth. He smiled at his executive assistant. "Two can play at this game. We have the budget and the power to force some of the influencers to change sides. If we play this right, we can begin to turn the tide and move thousands to our side."

"Sir, the MSS are masters of the web and social media, what if they do to us, what we're doing to them?"

"I believe they may have been doing this on a grander scale than us. I've declared total war on them."

"Yes, sir."

Torn nodded. "I know, we backed away for four years, which allowed them to jump in, and basically control the messaging on the Internet. Look at what they did with TikTok, they used it to mine millions of phones. If the reports we've received are true, they used the banking data they mined from the phones to fund the war against us. In a way, our citizens are funding the war against themselves. Two can play at that game."

Torn called his financial team leader. "I want you to get inside their banking network, and take all you can grab."

"Sir, you're asking us to be bank robbers?"

"No. I'm ordering you to rob and give back, say, with a bonus for their pain and suffering 25% more than our citizens lost. Then mark our debt as paid. If you're as good as you've told me you are, trillions of our debt will disappear as will billions of the money they stole from our citizens."

"Yes, sir. I understand. We'll get right on it."

Torn smiled as his aide handed him a fresh mug of coffee. "You've learned the Navy runs on coffee. I may be landlocked, but at heart I'm still an Admiral."

"Sir, you steer this ship through the rough seas to victory."

Torn smiled. "Thank you. I do have a few tricks left to play. This game isn't over yet. The MSS thinks they outsmarted us, that's only because I decided to hold my hold cards close to my chest. The assholes wanted war, well, now they're going to get one. We never announced any of the AI advances we'd made over the previous five years. Our friend downstairs is going to teach them a lesson."

"Sir, thank you. If there's anything I can do to help..."

"If I need your help, you'll be the first to know it."

Torn smiled when his assistant left. *We launched our worm into their sites two days ago, and it's already bearing fruit. If the damn thing works as designed, we can give them a taste of their own medicine. I wish we'd started the program earlier. They caught us with our pants down. The first time we got caught like this, the Japanese pulled us in World War Two. That didn't end so well for them. The second time caused us twenty years of bloodshed in the Middle East, the results being that, after all of the blood and lives lost, the situation in the sandbox is almost as bad as we found it twenty years ago. I hope that this time we've finally learned, and we don't leave ourselves open to getting hit a fourth time. We need to finish the job and never allow anyone to hit us like this again. We were fools to allow our potential enemy to own farms or any land close to our most important bases. My neighbor, who is Jewish, taught me something. He had it engraved into a brick from Auschwitz that he gave me. It says, "Never Forget/Never Again." I keep the brick in a glass case on my desk. If I have a say, we will destroy China's ability to wage war over the internet. If our new system is as good as I've been told, we're going to surprise the Chinese and teach them a lesson they'll never forget.*

Chapter 15
Site R, The Joint Chiefs' War Meeting.

The Raven Rock Mountain Complex, also known as Site R and simply The Rock, is a U.S. military installation with an underground nuclear bunker near Blue Ridge Summit, Pennsylvania, at Raven Rock Mountain that has also been called an "underground Pentagon." The bunker has emergency operations centers for the United States Military and the Department of Homeland Security. There is a war room very similar to the one under the Pentagon. The four chiefs of America's military sat around a metal table that was bolted to the concrete floor. The Chief of Staff looked around the table. "It seems like we haven't been here for 87 years, and from where I'm sitting, we didn't learn a damn thing.

"Back in '41we knew what the Japanese had planned before their own ambassador did. We'd broken the code, and then we didn't take advantage of what we knew. We didn't even trust our own president to know what we'd learned. We screwed around and didn't warn Pearl. Had we warned Pearl, they could have sortied the fleet and sunk their carriers before they launched their first plane. The Battleships could have hit them before they began their attack. The war would have been over before it started.

"We should never have allowed the Chinese or anyone to buy up land next to and in some cases surrounding our bases. How the hell were we so stupid? Don't anyone answer that. Here's what I figure, we need secure comms with the President. We need an inventory of what we have left and how we are going to hit them back. We also need to get Admiral Torn here. I'm sure he's busy but if anyone can figure out how to shove this war up the asses it's him. Comments?"

The CNO, Admiral Paul Slapp, spoke. "We're losing the war in the Pacific. They easily figured out our weakness and used it against us."

The general in command of the US Army looked confused. "You have weaknesses in your fifteen-billion-dollar ships?"

Slapp slowly nodded. "I'm sorry to say we've lost both of them. One in a traditional naval battle and the other by an EMP strike that shut down the ship. It was then a sitting duck."

The Chairman shook his head. "I know we discussed the threat of EMPs with the ships that were all electronic. I thought we agreed to move ahead with the changes HII proposed. What the hell happened?"

Slapp slowly nodded his head. "General, we did agree we required the fix HII proposed, but Congress didn't agree with us. They didn't understand EMPs and said if we got into a nuclear war, the EMPs would be the least of our problems."

"Damn it, please tell me the fool who said that got his."

"We don't know yet."

The Chairman looked around the table, "Who in the Lord's good name is the designated survivor?"

Slapp looked at the Chairman. "General, he was playing hearts with the Secret Service in the White House. They thought it would be a safe place. I don't remember us receiving a warning from our intelligence agency. You know, those people in Virginia who missed every major world event in the past fifty years. The President was right; he should have been allowed to close it and start over. Until the Speaker is well enough to take the oath, we're it, so I think we'd better start acting as the country's leaders. The other fact we have to face is, no one is coming to help us.

"I propose we withdraw from every treaty after we bring every bit of equipment we have and every member of ours home. We're going to need them here. I just learned a retired Marine LT Colonel led two hundred armed citizens against a Chinese farm then he led them against another. That's the spirit we need. I propose we appoint him to be the commander of the militia."

Marine General and Commandant of the Marines smiled. "That was LT Colonel Yamata. He never retreated. He served four tours in the Sandbox. His people would walk through Hell for him."

The Chairman nodded. "All who agree to reinstating and promoting LT Colonel, retired, to active duty as LT General and commander of the militia, which, per the Second Amendment, will be composed of every able-bodied armed citizen. All agree, raise your right hand."

All raised their right hand. "Now all we have to do is get the message out and get him here so we can brief him. Do we have any SEALs around who can sneak through the Chinese and locate him?"

The Army Chief of Staff said, "We have the twelve members of Detachment Delta upstairs. We can send them. We can print out a copy of Yamata's file that has his picture so they can locate the right person. I'll have his data loaded in one of the portable Biometric readers so we're sure it's the real Yamata and not a Chinese imposter. Keep in mind, I've read his file, he might laugh at the promotion and keep the Deltas."

The Marine general laughed. "I know him very well. If he's in the middle of attacking the Chinese he won't leave his people. I think we should ask the Deltas to confirm his ID, then brief him on the situation."

The Chairman nodded. "Give them the device and what we know and ask Captain Rubin Gallow, the commander of the A team, to locate him, and if Yamata can't or won't come to us, then he is to follow his orders. Gallow accepted the mission. He traded their new M7s for M4s. When asked why, he smiled. "There are trillions of rounds out there for the M4s, almost none for the M7 that fires a larger round. 6.8X52 vs the M4/AR 15 that fires the 5.56X45 round. We won't be able to carry enough rounds and mags if we took the M7s. If we took the M4s we will be able to share what Yamata and his people are using."

The CNO smiled. "A very good idea. I approve. May God go with you."

After sending Delta to retrieve or brief Yamata, they regrouped in the war room. The Chairman slowly nodded. Does anyone know the Speaker's condition, because we need a president? There are some things we can't do without his approval and code. Speaking of which, where's the fuc-en'Football?'"

The chiefs looked at each other. The Air Force Chief said. "One is at NORAD, one was at the Pentagon, and one with the Major at the ceremony and on Marine One with the President."

The CNO slowly nodded his head. "So we're down to one football with a President in Walter Reed and us sitting under a damn mountain. Hell of a way to run a war. Where is the previous President? Has anyone heard from him? I heard a rumor he's flying in circles over the Atlantic."

The Chief of Staff for Air Force replied. "He is. We have two F-16s escorting him. There's also a KC-135 and an E-2D with him. Before anyone asks, his plane was modified for air-to-air refueling. He made sure his plane could suck gas from either of our systems. By the way, he paid for the modification out of his pocket. It took

Boeing eight months to make the changes and upgrade the decoys and chaff on the plane."

The Chairman shook his head. "Why didn't he warn us?"

The CNO slowly stood. "He did, and he might have saved us. He used the little time he had left in office to move us to DEFCON 2. Our phones were off, and we handed our pagers to our staff. May I remind you that you ordered all of us to leave when one of your aides whispered the change of DEFCON to you. He knew something was about to happen, and he tried to warn us. What did you think he'd do, stand up and scream? 'We're under attack!' You know the media would have cut him off before the sentence was out of his mouth. I turned my phone and pager on when we were in transit here. He did send us a warning. It was pretty detailed and we, not him, blew it."

The Chairman slowly nodded. "What do you propose we do?"

"I know the President, he's not going to land here. He believes he's safe flying in large circles. His personal plane has jammers, decoys, and chaff launchers. He's safer where he is than down here with us."

The Commandant of the Marines asked. "Would he still have a football? It sounds like something he would do."

The Chairman nodded. "Let's see if we can speak with him. I too know him; he'll tell us the truth if we can reach him. I'll assume his plane still has the encrypted radios, let's see if the radio techs can reach his plane."

While they waited, the Chairman asked each chief for an accounting of their forces. The Marines went first. "We are prepared to carry out any orders. My Marines are always ready. When the President changed the DEFCON status, we prepared. The alert went out to every Marine base, ship, and to those on leave. In California, the Marines have taken up positions to protect the Naval Station San Diego and the airport. Many of those with Yamata are retired Marines.

"The corps at 29 Palms are moving to take up defensive positions at the Port of Long Beach. I have ordered some to protect the ground-based interceptors at Vandenberg. I pray we don't need them, but like insurance, it's better to have them and not need them, but need them, and not have them."

"Excellent work. CNO, you're next."

"We've lost our two newest carriers."

The Air Chief shook his head. "I remember discussing the design of the Ford Class. Every new technology on those boats was susceptible to EMP. The Nimitz Class used steam to launch planes. Had one of them been attacked by the EMP weapons, they would still be in the war."

The CNO slowly nodded. "I remember our discussion. It turns out you were right, but it's too late now. At last count, we've lost over twenty destroyers and most of the LCS boats. We've also lost most of our replenishment ships. The Chinese quickly figured out that when our surface ships ran out of missiles, they had to withdraw. We knew this weakness and must have had a hundred ideas how to overcome the issue. We spent hundreds of millions developing various systems to reload the vertical launch silos on the water. When we first developed the VLS, three of them held a reloading crane that could lift missiles from our replenishment ships and remove the empties and replace them with loaded cells.

"In our haste to increase the number of missiles, we removed the cranes and replaced them with three regular cells. We had made our problem worse. We then spent years in a hundred studies how to do what we used to have. We finally developed a system to reload ships at sea. We only had one, and it's now on the bottom of the Pacific.

"Our ships can't rearm and refuel anywhere in the Pacific without the replenishment ships that appeared to be the PLAN's primary targets along with our carriers. With the loss of our bases in the Pacific, our ships have to travel to Diego Garcia or back to San Diego to refuel and rearm. Without defensive weapons, we're losing ships we can't replace. They suckered us with hundreds of drones, which we used up our multi-million-dollar missiles to knock down their cheap drones, then, when our quiver was empty, they hit us with cruise missiles and ballistic missiles they called carrier killers, and they were. Without the fully armed destroyers, our carriers have to stay out of the range of their ballistic missiles. We have to refuel our planes on their approach and return."

The Chairman asked. "What about our submarines? I thought you started using unmanned drones to refuel your planes."

The CNO answered. "The Chinese target our refueling drones so our planes can't reach their targets or return to rearm."

"So our multi-billion-dollar Navy is useless against the Chinese? What a waste. Let's then discuss how we can hurt them."

The CNO smiled. "We hurt them the same way we defeated the Japanese almost 90 years ago. We use our submarines to sink their ships carrying the oil and raw materials they need. We starve them. We have the ability to kill their rice crops. Without raw materials and oil, their war machine will die. Without rice, their people will die. We know how to starve their people, I propose we use the weapon we swore to never use."

The Chairman clapped his hands. "Don't you think they have studied us and how we would respond to this attack? They know that since they didn't use WMD, we wouldn't. They know, the entire world knows we developed 'Agent Orange' to deforest Vietnam, the results of it are still with us today. If you're thinking about using 'Agent Black' you must think we have already lost. Some would consider 'Black' to be a WMD allowing them to respond in kind. That could lead to an all-out nuclear war."

"Not if they can't prove it was us. They have a lot of neighbors who are pissed at them. Maybe one of them managed to fly a series of small drones over a few of their large farms with a warning to stop the war or face starvation?"

"Admiral. Good plan, except they'll never buy we weren't behind the attack. I don't think they'll buy that one of their neighbors, just happened to have developed something like Agent Orange, only much deadlier to everything that grows and if I remember the report, it poisons the soil, rice paddy from being able to support anything from growing there again. That's a WMD if I ever saw one. We're talking about the starvation of a billion people."

"General, there is one who would know how to make a plant poison because they were on the receiving end of Agent Orange."

"You really think Vietnam will agree to take the fall for it?"

"We won't know until we ask."

The Marine general laughed. "It's nuts, but if our subs can sink their supply ships and the Agent Black hits their farms, they will be facing a citizen uprising. It would be helpful to have some SpecOps who speak Mandarin teach them how to overthrow their local mayor or whatever they call him. As long as our fingerprints aren't on the spray, they can believe it was us, but they'll have no proof. I like the crazy plan. We need to force them to change their focus until we get our troops home. If I remember correctly, Black is in spray bottles. Our SpecOps can spray a few farms as a message. I'm sure that when their rice crops start dying, they'll be ready to talk."

The Chairman nodded, "We have 84,000 people in Europe to be a speed bump for when the Russians cross the border, something they didn't do when they had some real advantages over us. I've said for a long time that it's time the Europeans pay for their own security. The question is, how do we bring them and all of their equipment home? We can't afford to leave the equipment behind like we did in Afghanistan.

The CNO said. "We can take over cruise ships and our heavy lift ships that brought the equipment to Europe in the first place, but we'll need escorts for them so the Chinese don't sink them and we lose our best people. I feel the Admiral's pain in how to reload and refuel his ships. I remember when I was a butter-bar and I asked my captain how the ship we were on would rearm and refuel if the replenishment ships were sunk."

The Chairman smiled. "What did your captain say?"

"He told me to keep such thoughts to myself and pray those ships never get hit. It was the main reason they were always kept out of the active war area. Since the only way we were going home was those ships who were waiting for us without any escorts, I felt naked and there was a large target over my head. There's no way an enemy wouldn't know those ships were our life preservers. If I was the enemy, I'd have my subs sink them and then run and hide to hit us while we were slowly trying to conserve our fuel to get home."

The Chairman nodded he looked at the Marine. "What would happen next?"

"I'd sink our escorts and then hit us since we would have no way to not only defend ourselves, but we wouldn't even know we were about to die until their fish exploded under our keel."

"You should have transferred to the Navy."

"I don't like swimming with my pack and weapon."

The Chairman nodded his head. "I propose we see if our subs can sink their tankers and freighters in the Indian Ocean. If we're really lucky, we might also sink a few of their boats. Who knows someone in Vietnam who can keep their mouth closed?"

The Marine General said. "My father had a contact in their military from his days over there. They became friends after the war. I'll have a little chat with him."

The Chairman said. "You're not leaving the bunker. Find a different way to get a message to your father. Does he know anyone in your command?"

"No, but he would know it's me if I use a code to start the message."

"Excellent. So, if you had been captured, he would know if the message was really from you. Send it with one of your most trusted people."

"General, I trust every one of my Marines with my life."

"I should have known that would be your answer. Send your message. I'm afraid we're running out of time. My darkest fear is that Russia takes advantage of us and either joins China or decides that, after almost 90 years, the time to take over Europe has arrived. They'll be watching our troop withdrawal with smiles. They know Europe can't stop them without using nukes, and the two countries who have them won't use them because they're afraid of the counter punch. We have no friends in this fight. I think we have to show China we still have some teeth."

The Air Force general asked. "Sir, if the Russians see us packing up and leaving and we all know they'll know. I think they'll wait till our people are home before they act and I agree, they will try to roll over Europe."

The CNO asked. "When they declare Article 5?"

The Chairman smiled. "Screw them. They refused to help us. Let them stew in their Europe knows better."

The other chiefs nodded their agreement. The Chairman continued. "They can't have it one way, either they honor our request, which they didn't, or screw them. I have a couple of questions. "Can your B-21s get inside China without being seen? Admiral, where do we stand on the quick strike weapons and the hypersonics in your three stealth destroyers?"

The Air Force general went first. "Sir, they can. What are you thinking?"

"Can we turn their lights out?"

"The EMP cruise missiles can be launched from the Raiders. I also believe we need to get Admiral Torn here, and I don't believe he'll leave Fort Meade. He has encrypted comms. I bet he's working on turning their lights out."

The Chairman nodded, "Let's get Torn on the line, if we have to hit them, then I want the following cities targeted, Beijing, Hong Kong, and Shanghai."

The Air Force general smiled, "General, I'd like to suggest we drop a few incendiaries on their forests, create a massive firestorm that will drain their manpower. We can mix in some WP bomblets so their water won't do shit, and if any of them are unlucky enough to get some on themselves, they'll be screaming till they pass out."

"Approved, but we want people wounded, not killed. We want to overload their medical infrastructure. Leave the network outages to Torn, set China on fire. I have a question for the Marines. If I can convince India to strike China, can you lend them, say, 10 or 20 thousand people and equipment?"

"I like it. Why not also Vietnam? We can hurt them from any direction they look."

The Chairman didn't have much faith in the CNO. He promised himself he'd speak to the President after he recovered. "Admiral, get your reserve fleet back in the war. Last time I saw your report, there were seventeen replenishment ships in the reserve fleet. I don't want to hear that those ships aren't capable. You sucked up millions that could have been used for additional resources, so show me that those ships are able to contribute to the war. You have over thirty destroyers, and of course, there's the cruisers you just retired. Get them into the fight."

"Yes, sir." The CNO whispered to his aide, who quickly left the conference room.

A moment later, Admiral Torn said through their encrypted comms. "Afternoon, sirs. How are you enjoying the first day of the Third World War. Einstein was asked about the Third World War. He said, 'he didn't know what weapons would be used in the Third, but he knew the weapons of the Fourth, rocks and sticks.' I've ordered a massive denial of service across their networks. I've also ordered our debt erased and every penny they stole from our people restored with a bonus. Our worms are in their networks. I had planned on activating them at midnight their time in Beijing, that's if you agree with my plan."

The Chiefs laughed. The Chairman said. I should have called you first. How confident are you that you can break their knees?"

"Sir, I know you were briefed on our advancement, so I'm one hundred percent sure."

The Chairman asked. "It works?"

"Better than any of us thought it would. It's busy right now, duplicating itself across their many networks."

The Chiefs looked confused. Torn asked. "Sir, may I brief them?"

"Yes. They now have a need to know."

"Sirs, as you know, the NSA is the world's largest user of what was called supercomputers. We began five years ago to develop real AI. I don't mean those simple versions Google and Facebook offered. I mean real machine learning and the ability to plan. It's been one of our darkest secrets. It is currently active, and at Midnight, he will turn the Chinese networks off. He has gotten into their banking system, the PLA's network, their leadership network, and their citizens' network. In a few hours, Xi is going to learn a very important lesson. He picked the wrong country at the worst of all times. We never forgot December 7th, we never forgot September 11th, and we're not going to ever forget January 20th.

"I know you're just itching to release your billion-dollar toy, the B21s, but my advice is to wait and see if my boy can do what he promised me he can do. Once the Chinese are blind and can't communicate with their forces, then you can strike their naval bases and ships. Leave their grid to us. If you use EMP weapons, they will too. My suggestion is to hold the EMP weapons back, but one hundred percent hit their Navy and every one of their air force bases along their border. Hit and destroy their DF 26 and 30 launchers. We can split the work."

The Chairman smiled. "Torn, you're always up for some fun, aren't you?"

"Sir, the bastards stole every penny my daughter had. Every penny my late wife left her is gone. It's personal to me now. My boy is ready. He's already fighting and winning. They never saw anything like him, and they didn't see him coming."

The CNO asked. "Why do you call it your boy?"

Torn smiled. "I designed the neural network. I designed his matrix and how he learns so I feel like he's my son. One I never had because my wife died when the drunk driver hit her head on because he was driving without lights on the wrong side of the road. My boy has shown my team every one of China's networks and where their server farms are. If you want a real target, then destroy their servers. Even if they managed to get some power back, they'll lose everything stored in their servers, and they won't be able to do shit on the internet. I've been waiting since the MSS fed their TikTok to millions of our citizens to teach them a lesson."

The Chairman looked at the other chiefs, each smiled and nodded. The Chairman asked Torn. "Can your boy send us the location of their servers?"

"He can and is even proposing the best weapons to destroy them."

The Air Force general smiled. "One day, I'd like to meet your boy."

"Any time."

The orders were sent to the B-2s and B-21s, along with the weapons to be used on each target. Some of the bombers were going to have to fly deep into China to take out three of the Chinese server farms. The good news was by the time the bombers arrived in China, the NSA should have blinded them.

Chapter 16

America Strikes Back.

Major Charles 'Chuck' Wilgrow had flown the B-1, B-2, and was one of the first to be promoted to be a command pilot in a B-21 Raider. He had hundreds of hours flying the B-21. He and his copilot, Captain Frank Rings, inspected the plane and checked the bomb load. They checked the surface of the plane to make sure there weren't any areas that could increase their radar signature.

Wilgrow climbed into the cockpit and checked the encrypted connection that was their link to NORAD. The radios used micro short bursts to overhead satellites that relayed the data to NORAD. Wilgrow typed a short message, 'Test Alpha. Raider flight of six ready to go."

"Confirm, you are green, repeat green."

Wilgrow told the other five crews they were good to go and were to maintain radio silence, except in an emergency. They took off and climbed to fifty thousand feet. They had no escort fighter flying with them. There was an AWACS over Canada that could watch them through their burst radios. The Canadian government told the Americans to stop flying in their airspace. The Canadian Prime Minister had received a special thank you from the Chinese to close their airspace to any American planes.

After taking off, the B-21s flew in different directions to confuse any Chinese spy watching. They also turned their transponders off, so they disappeared from anyone's radar. With the airspace over the United States being closed to commercial and private flights, there was no threat of running into a passenger flight.

Four B-1s took off minutes after the stealth bombers. They turned north and flew at treetop height. Their targets were Canada's major air force bases. The bombers flew down the runways while dropping runway cratering bombs that had a steel nose and a small rocket motor that enabled them to burrow into the thick runways before exploding, leaving a huge crater behind. Some incendiary bombs targeted the fuel tanks, which exploded like a small nuke. Canister bombs dropped hundreds of small bomblets over Canada's fighters. When the smoke cleared, Canada had lost the use of their air force bases, their badly needed jet fuel, and thirty F/A-18s it had purchased from Australia after it had switched to F-35s, and then, being angry at America's tariffs they decided to cancel their order for the F-35s.

The Chairman of the Joint Chiefs sent a message to the Prime Minister. "You used to be one of our best friends. We shed blood together. Since you have officially sided with the country that attacked us, you are now considered an enemy. An enemy that will learn what a serious mistake you'd made."

At that moment, the NSA's AI agent that had easily hacked the Canadian grid, Canada went dark. Their access to the internet was cut. Their water conditioning centers stopped. Even their street and traffic lights went dark. People panicked. The government couldn't even communicate with their citizens to tell them what had happened.

Every time the Canadians thought they had the fix to turn the power back on, the NSA's AI slammed the door closed in their faces. It's very cold and dark in Canada in late January. The Prime Minister never expected the Americans would turn on him. The American border patrol closed the Northern border. Canadians who attempted to flee Canada learned they were stuck in the cold and dark. They were told the blame was their Prime Minister's for siding with China over their neighbor. Neighbors are supposed to be friends and help protect each other. The Chairman reached his counterpart in Canada, he told her, "You are not considered a friend any longer. Any breach of our border will be considered an act of war. Stay on your side and allow our citizens who may wish to return to do so. If you attempt to use force, we will destroy your little socialist dream state."

The Prime Minister begged for forgiveness. He never thought his neighbor would slap him. "When will you turn our power back on?"

"We have no intention of returning the power until you surrender."

"What will happen if I decide to surrender?"

"Then you won't be the Prime Minister, and at which time we'll announce our plans for Canada. I can tell you that after the stunt you pulled, we no longer trust you. Your country will be broken up into states, and we will absorb your country."

"What if my people don't want to be Americans?"

"Then they can leave. We need our friends to have our back. You stuck a knife in our backs, and we will never forget such people."

The Chairman smiled and disconnected the call. He smiled at the Chiefs, "I guess he wet his pants. He thought he was dealing with a limp wristed government that, of course, would never cross them. The NSA is finding ways to inform the Canadians why they don't have any electricity and whose fault it was. I'm sure the Prime Minister is going to quickly retire before his people reach him."

*****

Based on Wilgrow's experience with the Raider, he had been given the task of developing their attack profile. His attack plan was designed to confuse the PLAAF if they were caught on China's defensive radars, which he had been promised would be done. If the attack on China's grid failed, he would be recalled. The Raiders didn't breach China's airspace; they launched their cruise missiles from 50,000 feet and fifty miles outside of China's airspace.

This was the first time the Advanced Attack Missiles (AAM) had been used in anger. The missiles were themselves stealthy, and they had small decoys they dropped behind them and jammers to further confuse China's tracking or missile radars. The B-21s had proven their radar invisibility in tests at the Air Force's test ranges. Their radar cross-section was 0.1M2, similar to a flying insect, invisible to radar. At one hundred from their release point, Wilgrow received the 'GO' code.

The AAM's radar signature was smaller than an insect. Each missile was assigned to one of China's massive server farms and electrical plants that provided the power to keep the servers running around the clock.

The missiles' nose cones were made of depleted uranium and covered with RAM to allow them to breach reinforced walls while also being invisible to radar. The missiles dropped small bomblets as they flew over the power plants. These destroyed most of the generators and large capacitors. Along with the bomblets were a handful of WP canisters that caused fires that destroyed the plants.

Before the bombers turned for home, they launched eight stealth cruise missiles that carried incendiary warheads. Their target was the large and very dense central forest. The weapons planners said the fires would pull enough oxygen into the center of the fires to create a firestorm that would suck the oxygen from the surrounding villages. It had been a hot and dry summer and a winter without any snow in the forests. The underbrush and dried leaves made for a perfect tender. The fires raced through the forests. The dense dark smoke was carried by the wind, as were hot embers that quickly spread the fire.

The missiles' last act was to crash through the walls of the server farms, spreading incendiary bomblets that ignited a fire that consumed the servers and all their data. The bombers managed to destroy seven power plants and eight server farms before they turned to return home. The bombers were met with a refueling plane and six F-22 Raptors and six F/A-18 Hornets fighters. The Hornets had a special mission. They each carried two AIM-174 air-to-air missiles. These had a range of over three hundred miles. The PLAAF's AWACs plane caught the refueling plane and fighters waiting for the bombers. They scrambled twelve J-20 stealth fighters to attack the bombers they knew the support planes had to be waiting for.

The Chinese came under attack before they left their own airspace. The American E-2D had seen the J-20s as they took off. The J-20 was an old design, one that the Americans had modified their early warning radar planes to deal with. They passed the data to the Hornets, who downloaded the targets to their AIM-174 missiles. The Chinese thought they had the longest-range air-to-air missile. They knew of the plane-carrying version of the Navy's ship-launched SM-6, but they thought there were very few in the fleet. The J-20s were quickly knocked down before they had entered their engagement range. The B-21s were refueled and all turned to return home. The E-2D and four Raptors led the way across the Pacific.

Beijing was furious. Their servers, their networks were down. 60% of their electrical power supply had been destroyed. The PLAAF knew, but couldn't prove, that the American stealth bombers had struck China. They wanted permission to use their bombers to strike America's grid. The Central War Committee didn't think the idea of sending bombers into America was a safe plan. One of the PLAAF generals reminded the committee they 'owned' Canada and would be inside America before their bombers would be discovered.

Xi was also informed that their networks were all offline, and even their encrypted radios were dead. While Xi was trying to understand the crash of their networks, an aide told him the country's ATMs were spitting out money. Just shooting out until they ran dry, and there were rumors of massive power failures and a forest fire.

Xi told his aide to make sure the local party chairmen handled the fires and power failures. He didn't believe the ATMs just spit out cash.

Xi dismissed his aide and returned to listen to the conversation about the Canadian Prime Minister. Part of their war plan was the closing of the Canadian airspace to the American bombers. The PLAAF told Xi the Americans had bombed the Canadian air force bases, so there would be no risk of flying over the pole and across Canada. Xi knew that if the Americans had attacked their long ally, they knew of the bribe and would have taken over the radar sites searching for planes crossing the pole. The MSS said their agents reported American fighters flying over the over the horizon radar sites.

Xi then spent two days looking at images of Canadian bases and damage done to the American bases on the first day of the war. He didn't have up-to-date images because the Americans had either destroyed China's spy birds or had used thought to be dead birds to push the Chinese birds out of orbit. He didn't know the Americans had backup birds in high orbits that were the backup in case of a war; their normal birds were taken out of service.

He ordered the PLAAF to fly their fastest plane equipped with a camera to get up-to-date images of the damage to America. The plane crossed the pole, and while it was being refueled, a long-range air-to-air missile was fired by a Raptor who was patrolling the north. The Chinese plane had been picked up by the Over-the-horizon radar site that the American Army had kicked the Canadians out of. The refueling plane exploded while the fighter was being refueled. The explosion of the larger plane sent burning debris into the fighter that destroyed both of its engines.

Xi asked the commander of the PLAAF. "Why didn't we spot and destroy their bombers? What if they had been carrying nuclear weapons?"

"Sir, it appears they didn't enter our airspace. They launched a new cruise missile that destroyed many of our power plants and, of course, the server farms that operate our networks and our access to the Internet. Our networks are down, all of them, our power is either down or rotating, so we can't keep the radars up."

XI was furious, "We're completely offline?"

"Sir, that is correct. The MSS was sending specialists to review the damage to the farms to see what, if anything, could be saved. We lost the server farms and the power plants."

Xi's face turned red. He was angry at the MSS, and the Americans. "How did they reach the farms deep inside our country if they didn't enter our airspace?"

The weapons expert from the MSS said. "They used a nuclear-capable missile that must have been one of their stealth cruise missiles. They invested billions in stealth designs."

Xi pointed at one of the guards and then at the PLAAF general. An almost silent gun fired from fifteen yards and blew the general's head apart.

Xi looked around the room. "Does anyone else want to make a stupid comment? Everyone knows they invested billions in stealth. We stole most of their designs. I don't remember anyone saying, 'Oh, look, stealth cruise missiles with different warheads. The only reason why we're not sitting in the dark is that this shelter has an underground generator. If we lose power, it means one of you is a spy and you and your family will pay the ultimate price."

One of the PLA generals said. "Sir, we need to go back and check our agents' notes to see if we missed anything."

Xi nodded. "Now that's what I'd call a good initial plan. Unless someone has something meaningful to add. Anyone?" No one moved or said a word. " Then that's the end of this meeting. If we learn anything else, I'll call another meeting. Get back to your offices and figure out how to get us back online and power restored, and is the rumor about the ATMs spitting money factual?"

Xi had forgotten about the report of the growing fires in the central part of their country. The dense smoke was only just beginning to spread over the cities. The drain from the destroyed power plants strained the grid enough that three more sections of the country went dark. The district managers and mayors called on Beijing to restore a steady flow of electricity because their citizens were getting angry, and what was Beijing's plan to deal with the fires that were growing every minute?

Xi had no idea what the local chiefs meant when they had asked him for help to put out the fires. Surely each city and region had a well-equipped fire department. He remembered being asked to increase the budget for those villages close to the dense central forests.

Chapter 17
The Indian Ocean and Xi's Surprise.

The USS *Texas* had received a sonar and targeting computer upgrade six months before the war broke out. Her partner USS *New Jersey* was equipped with one of the Navy's new large unmanned underwater attack drones. The drone followed a search program searching for Chinese ships. Their intel told them the Chinese ships weren't escorted. The drone scanned the area around the ships to make sure they were in fact, not being escorted by Chinese submarines. The two submarines had received orders to locate and sink any Chinese ships they could locate in the Indian Ocean.

The drone reported that the coast was clear for at least five miles, other than the convoy. The Chinese ships were in a convoy of six ships, all cruising at 12 knots. There were three oil tankers and three freighters in a loose line. All six were riding low in the water; they were full. They were the targets for the two American submarines had been ordered to locate and sink. Their orders specified they were not to surface, nor were they to raise an antenna or periscope above the water, where an unseen satellite might see and classify them as American submarines. Their orders were very clear; they were to sink the ships without a sign that the sinking was due to anything done by an American asset. They were not to surface to provide aid to any survivors, while being against the rules of the sea, both captains understood why. The sinkings had to be an unsolved mystery. The drone used a new torpedo, one that the Chinese spies hadn't been able to identify because they were funded in the Navy's black budget.

New Jersey and *Texas* spoke to each other through a new short-range underwater blue laser. They agreed to use the drone to attack the first and last ships in the convoy. When both were burning out of control, they would order the drone to sink the other ships in order. Once the six were burning out of control, the drone came shallow and raised its secret RF antenna and engaged its new jamming mode that blocked the ship's calls for help. The sunken ships would be a mystery. They were to be the first of every Chinese ship that traveled through the Indian Ocean. Their orders were to ensure raw materials and oil didn't reach China.

After the six ships had slipped under the ocean, the *New Jersey* brought the drone back to rearm it. The rearming was performed by six SEALs who loaded the new small torpedoes into the ready tubes and into the auto-loading arsenal. The drone relied on a loading mechanism similar to those in tanks. Once rearmed, the drone was sent hunting. It could use much smaller torpedoes than the attack submarines because it fired them from a position that was very close to its targets, and the warhead used a new explosive. The drone's AI memory was loaded with *Jane's Naval Catalog of Ships* so that it could determine friend from foe.

The *Virginia* class boats used off-the-shelf servers that were upgraded every couple of years. The servers were modified and had passed the Navy's shock tests. Each boat in the class had side-scan sonars that, combined with the bow-mounted and 'tail,' gave the boats a 360-degree view of anything in the water. Both *Texas* and *New Jersey* had recently been updated with new software and more sensitive sonars. They were also the first boats to receive the Mark-48 Mod 7B torpedo, which was quieter than the previous model. It was also faster and had a longer range when fired in its normal mode versus its new super quick mode. The two boats were the best the American Navy had. They were the quietest, fastest, and deadliest boats in the world. They were considered to be a generation ahead of any Chinese boats they might encounter. The two boats and their drone, which was a force multiplier, kept track of every ship in the Indian Ocean. Eighteen hours after the sinking of the six ships, *Texas* informed *New Jersey* that another convoy was entering the Indian Ocean. This one was composed of eight ships and a frigate as an escort. The frigate's helicopter was using a dipping sonar to search for submarines.

Texas and *New Jersey* had the latest generation of anechoic tiles that absorbed the helicopter's sonar pings. The two boats slowly and silently rose and took up position in the thermocline to further hide themselves from the Chinese searches for them. *Texas* had a surprise for the Chinese helicopter: a submarine-launched subsurface-to-air missile. The small missile rose from the water and struck the helicopter, blowing it to pieces.

New Jersey was equipped with the updated version of the sub-launched Harpoon Block III anti-ship missile. It was loaded into one of the torpedo tubes and fired. The launch canister had some fins that brought it to the surface when the Harpoon's booster ignited, accelerating the missile so its jet engine started. The Harpoon flew just above the ocean's surface. Once stabilized, the Harpoon's radar located its target. The Harpoon can be programmed to strike the target ship at the waterline, or it can pitch-up and dive onto the ship. The pitch-up mode was designed to give the missile a greater chance of avoiding the target's close-in defense guns. One addition to the Block IIIs was a jammer tuned to the frequencies used by the Chinese and Russian close-in weapons.

The Chinese frigate's radar spotted the Harpoon as it rose from the surface. The captain sounded general quarters and ordered the ship's single 30mm close-in cannon to shoot down the missile. At the same time, he ordered decoys and chaff launched to confuse the missile's tracking radar. He didn't know the Block IIIs had been programmed to ignore the chaff and decoys, or if the missile's radar was jammed then it would switch its targeting to its thermal sensor. The Harpoon rose up and dove through the unarmored deck above the engines.

Five hundred pounds of an improved warhead destroyed the frigate's engines and generator. The blast also tore a hole in the ship's hull, breaking its keel. Water flooded into the destroyed engine room and put out most of the fires. The explosion and hull breach had slightly broken the keel, so none of the watertight doors were completely sealed. The water rushed into the ship, which, without power, couldn't begin to pump the rising water out. The captain tried everything he could think of to save his ship, but without power, he had no options, so he ordered the surviving crew to abandon the sinking ship. Most of the crew had been trapped inside the hull and drowned as the ocean flooded the ship.

The captain and fifteen of his crew managed to get off the ship before it completely surrendered to the cold water. They managed to swim to one of the bright orange rafts as the ship slipped under the water. One of the oil tankers sent a small boat to save the survivors of the frigate. As the survivors were being helped onto the tanker, three torpedoes from the unmanned drone exploded under its keel. The tanker was carrying jet fuel, it exploded like a small nuke.

The last ship in the convoy was loaded with fertilizer; it too exploded. The burning debris fell on the ship in front of the freighter. That ship was also an oil tanker. The burning debris and fumes from the refined gasoline fuel created an explosion that sent debris at over 100 Mph into the next ship that caught fire. The drone used up the last of its ready torpedoes to sink the last of the ships in the small convoy.

The frigate had managed to send a signal they were under attack by a submarine. The signal was picked up by a Chinese satellite that hung over the Indian Ocean. The message wasn't received in Beijing for over a week due to the blackout so the warning to the next two convoys wasn't delivered. The delay in receiving the warning cost the Chinese two additional convoys of a total of eighteen ships. Beijing was starting to run out of oil.

The blackout meant their early warning radars only functioned for a few hours a day on their generators. One radar site would operate for three hours, then the next would operate for three, and so forth. The Americans tracked the rolling operation of the radars and ordered a strike on China's vast oil storage and refining sites. An *Ohio-class missile submarine armed with six 'quick strike'* missiles (Trident nuclear submarine-launched missiles that had their warheads replaced with conventional explosive ones). Each missile carried four of the new warheads. The six missiles were launched through the window of no radar coverage and delivered a total of twenty-four warheads that destroyed the world's four largest oil refineries. The explosions and firestorm caught a dozen fuel trucks that had just been filled with fuel in the explosion. The trucks exploded like thousand-pound bombs. Their burning fuel added to the massive firestorm that engulfed seven small towns. When the firestorms left the towns, there weren't any survivors.

The blackouts also kept the message of the forest fires from being received by Beijing. Without sufficient manpower to fight the forest fires, they continued to grow. It took a week for a handful of generators to be installed in Beijing to power the Defense ministry and Xi's office and to power a small number of servers for urgent messages to be received in Beijing. Xi was shocked by the news he was being told. Six convoys had been sunk, plus three escorting frigates.

The forest fires had consumed over one hundred thousand hectares and were still out of control. The people in Hong Kong rebelled against the police and troops because of the lack of power, clean water and food. The air in Hong Kong was full of the harmful, dense smoke, and the fires were burning out of control. The PLA was keeping control of the citizens of Beijing, but large areas of the city had been burnt down when the firestorms destroyed the western part of the city, and the mobs looted a third of the city looking for food and clean water. The firestorm continued on its deadly course, it left only destruction and death in its wake.

Xi was furious. The Central Committee pressed Xi on stepping aside because the quick, painless war he and the MSS had planned was turning into a disaster. Cities were being destroyed, and in others, the citizens were tearing them apart because no food or fuel had been delivered. Without oil and fuel, rationing kept factories closed, leaving people without the money to buy food. Most of the country was without power. Some towns attacked PLA bases in search of food and water. That's when the news arrived in Beijing the rice crop was dying. It had started in the farms close to or in the new war zone.

Xi refused to resign peacefully. He threatened to have the ministers shot for treason. The Minister of Oil production and distribution smiled and nodded at Xi while he placed his hand in his pocket and fired a small 380 ACP into Xi's chest. The Minister pulled the small pistol out of his pocket and fired one round into Xi's head. He turned to the other ministers. "Now, I suggest we announce our beloved leader has suffered a sudden and fatal heart attack. I nominate our Secretary of State, Han Ho, to replace Xi. We need someone who understands the Americans more than Xi did. He led us into the war that might be the death of all of us. We either have to get America to surrender, or we have to come to a cease-fire agreement with them."

The committee elected Han Ho as the General Secretary of the Chinese Communist Party and President of China. His first job was to figure out who the American President was. He was told the Speaker of the House, who was still in the hospital, was sworn in as the President. He was told the new President had been poisoned with Novichok, that was a nerve agent. When Ho learned that the attempted assassination of the new president had been an operation by agents of the MSS, Ho was furious. He had met the Speaker. He knew he was a soft-spoken man who had a spine of pure steel. He knew he had to find a way to cool things down before the new President used their immense arsenal against China.

Ho ordered the MSS to locate and terminate the agent or agents in America who had carried out the mission. He sent a message to the new President through their ambassador. He was shocked when the ambassador informed him the president was very weak from the poisoning. He had announced his appointment for his Vice President. Ho spoke to the ambassador on an encrypted satellite phone. When the call ended, he fell backward into his large leather desk chair. His Minister of Defense asked him what was wrong.

The ambassador said. "We have more problems than we thought. Their president is very weak. He's recovering but isn't up to the heavy demands of running a war with us. He did something that surprised most of his citizens and the world. We're the last to know because of the blackout."

An aide rushed into the conference room. "Sir, we have a serious problem."

Han Ho looked at the aide. "How dare you interrupt us."

"Sir. I am very sorry, but I have some very serious news."

"Okay, be quick about it. What is the news?"

"India and Vietnam have declared war on us. Their troops are pouring across our borders."

Han Ho looked at his Minister of Defense. "Stop them!"

"Sir, we have no communications with our armies. Most of the country is without power, and there is a massive fire destroying the forests. We can't round up the people to fight the fires."

Han Ho shook his head. "I'm more worried about the Indians than the Vietnamese. Do you have any idea how deep their inclusion is? Do we have any armies that can stop them? Wait, you said the rice crop is dying in the combat zone, which combat zone?"

"Sir, the zone where the Vietnamese crossed our border. They either modified the old American chemical weapon they called Agent Orange or the Americans made a new and more deadly version and gave it to them. Either way, without the convoys and if they continue salting our rice crops, our people are going to starve, We know what that means, they will revolt. The PLA will have to use real bullets and they'll be killing our own people. Don't we have entire army groups along both borders? The Indians and us have been at each other's throats for years.

"No, sir. We pulled them from the border to prepare for the invasion of Taiwan. Many of them were killed in the strikes on their staging areas and when their ships were sunk."

Han Ho shook his head. "Call up the reserves."

"We can't without power. We have no internet because the server farms were all destroyed, and the Americans have blocked us from securing new ones."

"What about Russia?"

"They're still on the Americans' embargo list. No high tech can be shipped to us or them."

Han Ho smiled. "Wait, I know we had a backup server farm in the mountains one hundred Km from the Indian border."

The aide sadly nodded. "Sir, used is the correct term. The Indians knew the location and, after pulling the drives, they set fire to the facility, destroying the servers and the building."

"Do we have any other sites?"

"The other backup site, which was three times the size of our backup site that the Indians just destroyed, isn't responding either. It was very close, maybe 10 Km our border with Vietnam."

The Minister of State asked. "Sir, I'm sure we can make a cease-fire with whomever this VP is. Did our ambassador give you a name?"

The aide checked his notes. "Sir, he did. He told our ambassador the new VP and the one who is running America is none other than the person who was their 45th and 47th president."

Han Ho shook his head. "Oh shit. He hates us. He'd sworn that if anyone attacked America, he would completely destroy them, and he's leading the country until the person we tried to kill recovers? Does he know we were behind the poisoning of the President?"

The aide nodded. "He knows. He told our ambassador he should go home and kiss his wife and children goodbye, and he should send us a message that our days were numbered."

The Minister of Defense asked. "Can he do that?"

Han Ho nodded. "He can."

"I thought the Americans lost their nuclear release computer when we destroyed the Pentagon."

Ho shook his head. "We were wrong. One survived, and he has it. He told our ambassador he had already ordered every B-1 and B-52 that were stored to be put back into operation, along with anything else that can carry a bomb. He also told us that he's ordered their Trident missiles to be upgraded to carry ten warheads per missile, and he smiled when he told our ambassador he will end the CCP's reign of terror."

The Minister's face paled. He sat down and stared at the ceiling. "I think we need to call the entire committee back and discuss our options."

Han Ho shook his head in defeat. "I believe we might have only a couple of options, one, full all-out war with them, or surrender. Either way, we're doomed."

The Director of MSS nodded. "Then we have to remove him from his position. We might be able to get a better deal with the President. I learned he is gaining strength every day. We have to wait it out and not carry out the next phase of our attacks. The sooner their President recovers, the better our chances are of surviving."

The minister asked. "Do we have any idea how long we have to wait?"

An aide to the Minister of Defense shook his head. "I have no idea. I propose we move our ministers and their staff to the mountain, so if we do have to fight a nuclear war with the Americans, we'll be safe. There is one other issue we have to deal with; the PLA troops we sent to America are not responding to our calls."

Han Ho asked. "Is that bad?"

The minister nodded. "Very. They're on a clock. When their clock hits zero hour, they will attack."

Han Ho shook his head. "Oh shit. Did he say anything else?"

. "He looked our ambassador in his eyes and said in a very low voice. "Vengeance is mine." Then he smiled and told the Secret Service, who were armed with assault rifles, to kick our ambassador out of his office and out of the country."

Han Ho asked. "What's next?"

He looked around the conference room. No one else wanted to say a word. "I assume the quick war Xi and the MSS started is going to turn into a World War. One. I'm not sure we can win.

The Aide said. "He told our ambassador that since NATO decided to sit this one out, he has pulled their people and equipment back to America. He smiled when he said, now they're going to have something new to do."

Han Ho shook his head. "Then maybe we should stand by and let the PLA do what they do. We can deny all knowledge of their actions, and if the PLA does anything to further harm America, we can disown them as being new to our jobs. If only we could get a message to them. I'd tell them to find and kill the new VP."

The Minister of Defense shook his head. "We can try, but we both know he was just looking for a reason to destroy us, and we gave it to him on a silver platter. If, as our agents have reported, they managed to get fourteen of their missile boats out and there are battles being fought between armed citizens, their Army, and even their police officers have banded together to kill our people and return their silos to their control."

Han Ho sat down at the head of the table. "I believe we must do everything in our power to terminate him."

End of the War in 2029 Book 1

Book 2, War in The War in 2029, "Revenge is Mine" (Fall 2025)

Additional books by the author that are available on Amazon:

The War in 2029. Book 1
The War in 2029, Book 2. Revenge is mine, to be published fall 2025

We're Not Alone, Book 1
We're Not Alone, Book 2

Black Friday, Book 1, The Accidental Third War
Black Friday, Book 2, Building a New Community
Black Friday, Book 3, The Dark Times
Black Friday, Book 4, Reality Sets In
Black Friday, Book 5, The Uncivil War
Black Friday, Book 6, United We Stand
Black Friday, Book 7, Invasion
Black Friday, Book 8 The Aftermath
Black Friday, Book 9 The Truce
Black Friday, Book 10, The End

NATO's Article 5 Gambit Book 1
NATO's Article 5 Gambit Book 2
NATO's Article 5 Gambit Book 3
NATO's Article 5 Gambit Book 4
NATO's Article 5 Gambit Book 5

Buddy can you spare a few Trillion?

Behind Every Blade of Grass Book 1
Behind Every Blade of Grass Book 2
Behind Every Blade of Grass Book 3
Behind Every Blade of Grass Book 4
Behind Every Blade of Grass Book 5
Behind Every Blade of Grass Book 6
Behind Every Blade of Grass Book 7
Behind Every Blade of Grass Book 8
Behind Every Blade of Grass Book 9
Behind Every Blade of Grass Book 10

The Smoky Mountain Militia (A story set in the Behind Every Blade of Grass universe.)

Behind Enemy Lines. (Coming soon.) (A story set in the Behind Every Blade of Grass universe.)

The Wrath of God, Book 1
The Wrath of God, Book 2
The Wrath of God Book 3 (fall/winter of 2025)

Red Sunset
Earthquake
Pestilence
Pax Romana

It's Good to be the King. Book 1
It's Good to be the King, Book 2

The Changelings Book 1
Justin's Journal
Project Xiangqi
Korean Crises

CALEXIT, Book 1, Secession
CALEXIT, Book 2, Politics as Normal
CALEXIT, Book 3, If at First, You Don't Secede

America on Fire

37 Miles (Revised Edition)
37 Miles, Book 2, Patty's Journey

My Story
A History Lesson (Short story)

2015 Second American Civil War, Book 1
2015 Second American Civil War, Book 2
2015 Second American Civil War, Book 3
2015 Second American Civil War, Book 4
2015 Second American Civil War, Book 5

By the Light of the Moon, Book 1
By the Light of the Moon, Book 2

By the Light of the Moon, Book 3
By the Light of the Moon, Book 4

Christmas Eve

The Shelter, Book 1, The Beginning
The Shelter, Book 2, A Long Day's Night
The Shelter, Book 3, The Aftermath
The Shelter, Book 4, The New World.
The Shelter, Book 5, War
The Shelter, Book 6, Revenge
The Shelter, Book 7, Genesis
The Shelter, Chapter 2, A New Beginning

In the Year 2050, America's Religious Civil War
In the Year 2050, Book 2

The Impeachment of President Obama
Silent Death
The Third World War

We Knew They Were Coming, Book 1
We Knew They Were Coming, Book 2
We Knew They Were Coming, Book 3
We Knew They Were Coming, Book 4
We Knew They Were Coming, Book 5
We Knew They Were Coming, Book 6
We Knew They Were Coming, Book 7
We Knew They Were Coming, Book 8
We Knew They Were Coming, Book 9
We Knew They Were Coming, Book 10

Feel free to contact me at itabankin@aol.com with any questions or comments.

Printed in Dunstable, United Kingdom